# HBR Guide to Better Business Writing

# 哈佛商業評論 英文商務寫作權威指南

布萊恩 A. 賈納
Bryan A. Garner —— 著　賴榮鈺 —— 譯

作者序

# 本書學習重點

## What You'll Learn

你是不是一遇到要寫備忘錄給高階主管，就愣住不知該如何下筆？你的報告是不是亂無章法，讓主要利益關係人看了之後，產生的疑惑多過於解答？你寫給同事的電子郵件是不是像石沉大海，未收到回信也沒有後續動作？你的提案是不是總無法獲得客戶青睞？

如果不擅長於商業寫作，你損失的不只大量時間，還有可觀的金錢和影響力。而這是很多人都有的問題。我們許多人即使說話時清晰流暢，但一寫起文件，就會為了搜尋適當的詞彙和語氣而傷透腦筋。不過，情況其實可以有所不同。條理清楚且具說服力的寫作，需要的不是魔法，也不是運氣，而是技巧。本書除了給你信心，也提供培養這些技巧所需的工具。

本書將協助你提升以下技能：

- 突破寫作瓶頸。
- 組織你的想法。
- 清楚表達主要重點。
- 直接切入主題。
- 抓住目標讀者的注意力。
- 寫出簡潔實用的摘要。
- 精簡內容，幫文件瘦身。
- 寫得切中要點，恰到好處。
- 避免文法錯誤。

# 推薦序

寫作在臺灣是項常被忽略的技能，很多人認為只要把自己的想法寫出來，頂多再潤飾一下修辭，就大功告成。這樣的觀念延伸至英文寫作上，就容易誤以為只要字彙正確、文法無誤，就是一篇好文章。但寫作其實是個人內在思考的具體外顯，是非常複雜的認知過程。除了表達語意之外，還必須思考如何使訊息條理連貫、論點清晰嚴謹、風格吸引讀者，並使內容產生實質影響等，才能達到有效溝通的目的。

特別是在正式的商業寫作情境，書面文字更承載了展現專業素養、影響他人決策、促進協作效率、乃至於左右交易成敗等功能。換言之，商業寫作是種具有實質影響力的行為，其重要性不容低估。然而在國內，商業英文寫作的訓練似乎沒有受到足夠重視，而且大多仍著重在學習詞彙文法的層面，難以達到專業的品質，相當可惜。

在這樣的背景下，日月文化出版公司引進《哈佛商業評論英文商務寫作權威指南》（HBR Guide to Better Business Writing）就顯得格外有意義。這本書為「哈佛商業評論指南系列」（Harvard Business Review Guide Series）中的代表作。該系列專為現代忙碌的經理人所設計，涵蓋管理、溝通、領導、時間管理等眾多主題，且內容實用、篇幅精鍊、版面易讀，深受全球職場人士喜愛。

我個人很喜歡這本書的幾個特色，首先是全書章節編排的邏輯清楚：從分析寫作的策略出發，包括了解寫作目的與讀者、寫作流程四步驟、列出三重點、善用圖表等；接著說明如何培養寫作技能和避免不良寫作習慣，針對冗詞贅語、句型鬆散等常見問題提出修改建議；

再推進至各類商業文本的寫作實務，如電子郵件、信件、備忘錄、報告和績效考核表等；最後附錄裡還整理了寫作檢查清單與常用文法、標點、用語規則等。整本書為讀者提供明確而有系統的自學途徑。

其次，書中各章節採用大量中英對照的寫作範例，涵蓋重要的商務溝通場景如詢問進度、修改訂單、拒絕提案等，並依據不同目的提供不同版本，還呈現正確和錯誤的示例以供比較，協助讀者從實際例證中歸納寫作原則。我們還可模仿其英文句型和寫作格式，直接應用於各種職場寫作情境。

另外值得一提的是，本書原文是為英文母語者所編寫，換句話說，即便是英美經理人也需要本書提供的原則和技巧來改善自身的商業寫作。對我們英語非母語者而言，要在職場中以英文書寫更是難上加難。然而本書不僅有助於英文能力欠佳者提升寫作能力，也能協助英文能力良好的人士精進其商業寫作技巧。

簡言之，商業英文寫作之所以困難，並非只是因為它是外文，而是它還同時涉及商業情境、寫作策略、讀者需求與職場文化等多種因素，因此需要專業指引和技巧練習方能嫻熟駕馭。而與其在職場上透過摸索試錯（trial and error）這種缺乏效率的方式學習，不如馬上使用本書作為指南，展現你精準表達與有效溝通的技能，發揮在國際商場上的影響力。

廖柏森

臺師大翻譯研究所教授／英文寫作翻譯暢銷書作者

# 目 次

SECTION 3: Avoiding the Quirks That Turn Readers Off

## 避免怪異的寫作習慣讓目標讀者失去興趣



SECTION 4: Common Forms of Business Writing

## 常見的商業寫作形式



## 附錄

簡介

# 提升寫作技巧的必要性

## Why you need to write well

對於寫作，你可能會覺得不用太過講究，過得去就行了，但這樣的心態恐怕會讓你付出高昂代價。你的上司、同事、員工、客戶、合作夥伴，以及任何與你溝通交流的人，都會透過你的文字來認識你這個人。如果你的文字拙劣、馬虎，他們可能會假定你的思想也是如此。如果你無法說服他們應該看重你的訊息，他們也就不會把它當一回事，甚至可能認定你不是值得合作的對象。你為此賭上的風險就是這麼的高。

有些人會說寫作沒有什麼大不了，他們可能是覺得自滿，或是認為重要的是想法，寫作不重要。但先要寫得好，想法才會受人注意，進而才能實踐。所以，不要被誤導了，好的寫作確實很重要。

不擅寫作的人是在自己和讀者之間築起一道藩籬，擅長寫作的人則是搭起與讀者間的橋梁，啟迪其心智，以至達成目標。

要給人留下強烈印象，無論好壞，只要短短幾個字就能做到。以下列舉四段文字，其中兩段可有效傳達訊息，另外兩段則否。一起來看看你是否能分辨孰優孰劣：

1. In the business climate as it exists at this point in time, one might be justified in having the expectation that the recruitment and retention of new employees would be facilitated by the economic woes of the current job market. However, a number of entrepreneurial business people have discovered that it is no small accomplishment to add to their staff people who will contribute to their bottom line in a positive, beneficial way.

2. In this job market, you might think that hiring productive new employees would be easy. But many entrepreneurs still struggle to find good people.

3. The idea of compensating a celebrity who routinely uses social media to the tune of thousands of dollars to promote one's company by tweeting about it may strike one as unorthodox, to say the least. But the number of businesses appropriating and expending funds for such activities year on year as a means of promotion is very much on the rise.

4. Paying a celebrity thousands of dollars to pro mote your company in 140-character tweets may seem crazy. But more and more businesses are doing just that.

1. 在當前現有的商業氛圍之下，鑒於目前就業市場上的經濟不利情勢，一般人若認為招聘和留住新進員工會因此變得容易，這樣想似乎也很合理。然而，有些自行創業開公司的人發現，要以正面有益的方式，找到對公司收益有幫助的員工，絕對不是一件容易的事。

2. 你可能認為在現今的就業市場，要僱用高生產力的新員工並不困難，但對許多創業者來說，要找到理想員工仍非易事。

3. 付出高達數千美元的代價，請活躍在社群媒體的名人發佈推文來宣傳公司，再怎麼說，聽起來都不是正規的做法。但與去年同期相比，撥出及提高經費採取這種宣傳方式的公司，數量卻只增不減。

4. 支付數千美元請名人寫 140 字的推文來宣傳你的公司，聽起來可能很不可思議，但這正是越來越多公司在做的事。

你能看出差別嗎？當然可以。第一段和第三段的範文冗長又囉嗦，語法結構複雜，偶爾還會離題。第二段和第四段則是簡潔易懂，直接切中要點，絲毫不浪費對方的時間。

既然你已懂得分辨何為可有效傳達訊息的商業寫作，相信我，你也能學會寫出這樣的內容。你可能覺得寫作是件苦差事，很多人都有同感。但有些歷經時間考驗的方法，可降低寫作時的焦慮和辛勞。這就是本書要呈現的內容，同時附上大量「修改前」和「修改後」的範例，以示範如何實際應用這些方法。（這些範例皆取材自真實文件，但有稍加改編。）

擅於寫作不是與生俱來的天賦，而是和其他許多事物一樣，是後天習得的技能。任何具有一般運動天分的人，都能學會射籃或高爾夫球揮桿，達到還不錯的水準。任何具有一般智力和協調性的人，都能學會有模有樣的演奏某個樂器。而若你已經讀到這裡，相信在幾項指導方針的協助下，你也能學好寫作，或許還能寫得非常好。

## 把自己視為專業寫作者

如果你在工作上需要透過文字撰寫才能取得成果，不管所寫的是信件、提案、報告或任何內容，那麼你就是一位專業寫作者。廣義來說，你和記者、廣告撰稿人和書籍作家都屬於同一個類別：你的成敗可能很大程度取決於所產出的作品，以及對讀者的影響。因此，對於所寫的內容要盡可能再三的琢磨。

以下這個例子你可能有聽過。這個故事有許多版本，有時設定在不同的城市，故事轉折也略有不同：

> 一位盲人坐在公園裡，脖子上掛著一塊牌子，上面潦草的寫著「（I AM BLIND.）我看不見」，在他的前方擺著一個錫製的杯子。一位路過的廣告撰稿人停了下來，看到杯子裡只有七十五分錢，他問道「先生，可以讓我改寫你的牌子嗎？」。「但我這牌子是我妹妹照我所說的寫的。」「我知道，但我想我能幫上點忙。讓我寫在背面，你可以試一試。」盲人遲疑的同意了。結果過了不到兩個小時，杯子裡堆滿了紙鈔和硬幣。又有一位路人投錢時，盲人開口問道：「請等一等，我這塊牌子上寫了什麼？」投錢者回答：「只寫了七個字，『（It is spring, and I am blind.）春天來了，而我卻看不見。』」

由此可見，表達方式至關重要。

## 深入透徹的閱讀，學習好的寫作風格

若想要清楚的表達想法並說服他人，必須培養以下幾項特質：

- 時時謹記自己是為何而寫，別忘記目標讀者的需求。
- 堅決選擇以最簡單的詞彙來準確表達概念。
- 多用自然常見的慣用語。
- 避免使用行業術語和商務用語。
- 懂得根據場合、情境使用適當的詞彙。
- 可分辨不同語氣的差別。

這些特質要如何培養？首先，閱讀任何東西時，都別忘觀察內容是否符合這些特質。靜下心慢慢研讀專業作者的作品。別把這當成一項乏味的例行工作，也別等到漫長的一天結束，才硬擠出一點時間。利用早上喝咖啡的時間或工作間的空檔，撥出幾分鐘來仔細的閱讀。找到自己喜歡的理想素材，可以是《經濟學人》（the Economist）、《華爾街日報》（the Wall Street Journal），或甚至《運動畫刊》（Sports Illustrated）的文字也是極佳的素材。

如果可以，想像自己是新聞播報員，每天至少大聲唸出一篇文章。（沒錯，就是要大聲唸出來。）要有感情的唸，注意標點符號、遣詞用字、行文節奏以及分段的運用。這個習慣可針對你想學習的技能培養鑑賞力。訓練出這方面的意識後，唯一要做的就是練習。

## 了解可獲得的回報

一封語意不清的信件，需要反覆往返的更正資訊，才能釐清誤解，既耗費資源，也損及信譽。一份措詞不當、漏洞百出的備忘錄，可能會導致決策失誤。一份結構鬆散的報告可能會使重要資訊掩沒其中，而使目標讀者忽略重要的事實。一份冗長乏味的提案，只能落得被擱置一旁、遭人遺忘的下場。要給重要客戶的簡報，若是初稿寫得亂七八糟，高層主管還得在最後一刻花時間重寫一份過得去的簡報，結果因為準備工作做得忙亂，而使成功機率大打折扣。

這些不僅浪費許多時間，更拖垮了公司獲利。但只要透過簡潔明瞭的寫作，就能防止這一切問題。這不是什麼隱密、遙不可及的神祕藝術，而是一項不可或缺的商業工具。了解如何使用這項工具，以達成你所追求的成果。

事先說明：本書的例句如有任何英文文法、拼字或用法上的錯誤，皆會以星號（*）加以標註。

- Section -

# 1

# 清楚明快的完成寫作

Delivering the Goods Quickly and Clearly

第 1 章

# 了解自己為何而寫

Know why you're writing

很多人在還沒搞清楚要達成的目標之前，就已經開始動手下筆。結果就是讀的人不明白重點為何，也不知道該做些什麼。**寫作的內容絕大部分取決於寫作的目的，所以你必須時刻將目的牢記在心。**你想要達成什麼樣的成果？舉例來說，是要說服某人簽署加盟契約，還是停止未經授權使用你的商標，或是希望對方親自造訪公司？

以清楚且令人信服的方式說明問題，以及你想達成的目標。每寫一句，都問問自己是否離目標更近一步，這可協助你找到最適合的措詞以有效傳達訊息。

## 形式取決於目的

假設你的公司在一棟辦公大樓承租辦公室，該大樓的入口和一樓整層最近曾徹底整修。你的法律顧問提醒你，大樓房東違反了《美國身心障礙者法》（Americans with Disabilities Act，ADA），比如說，沒有輪椅坡道和自動門。因此你決定寫封信給房東。但你寫這封信的**目的為何**？這個問題的答案很大程度決定了你要寫的內容，更是**決定**

**這封信語氣的關鍵**。想想以下三種可能的版本：

## 版本 1

你和房東是好朋友，但你覺得為了員工和顧客的利益，該守的法律還是要遵守。目的：了解更多資訊。語氣：友善。

Dear Ann:

The new foyer looks fantastic. What a great way for us and others in the building to greet customers and other visitors. Thank you for undertaking the renovations.

Could it be that the work isn't finished? No accommodations have yet been made for wheelchair accessibility — as required by law. Perhaps I'm jumping the gun, and that part of the work just hasn't begun? Please let me know.

Let's get together for lunch soon.

All the best,

親愛的安：

新的門廳看起來棒極了，對我們和這棟大樓的其他用戶來說，這真是招待顧客和其他訪客最理想的地點。多虧了你做的這一番整修。

但整修是否仍未完工？因為目前沒有看到依法須鋪設的輪椅坡道。或許是我太過心急，這部分的作業只是還沒開始？煩請告知情況。

最近一起吃個午餐吧。

祝一切順心

## 版本 2

你和房東的關係良好，但原則上，你不希望公司所在的大樓違反法律規定。你的公司也有行動不便的員工，你希望這個情況可以獲得改正。目的：糾正這項疏失。語氣：較為急迫。

Dear Ann:

Here at Bergson Company, we were delighted when you renovated the first floor and made it so much more inviting to both tenants and visitors. We are troubled, however, by the lack of wheelchair-access ramps and automatic doors for handicapped employees and customers, both of which are required by state and federal law. Perhaps you're still planning that part of the renovations. If so, please advise.

If this was a mere oversight, can you assure us that construction on ramps and automatic doors will begin within 60 days? Otherwise, as we understand it, we may be obliged to report the violation to the Vermont Buildings Commission. Without the fixes, you may be subject to some hefty fines — but we feel certain that you have every intention of complying with the law.

Sincerely,

親愛的安：

在柏格森公司，我們很高興看到你把一樓重新整修，讓租戶和訪客都能享用更加舒適宜人的空間。不過，有一點讓我們感到困擾，因為沒有可供身障員工和客戶使用的輪椅坡道和自動門。依本州法律和聯邦法的規定，輪椅坡道和自動門都是必要設備。或許這部分的整修仍在規劃當中，若是如此，敬請告知。

如果這點只是一時疏忽，你是否能保證會在六十天內開始設置輪椅坡道和自動門？否則，就我所知，我們有義務向佛蒙特州建築委員會檢舉此違規事項。若未改善，即有可能面臨高額罰款，但我相信你一定非常樂意遵守法律。

謹啟

## 版本 3

你和房東曾經有過幾次糾紛，你已經為公司找到其他更好的承租地點。目的：終止租約。語氣：堅定但未撕破臉。

Dear Ms. Reynolds:

Four weeks ago you finished renovating the first floor of our building. Did you not seek legal counsel? You have violated the Americans with Disabilities Act — as well as state law — by failing to provide a wheelchair access ramp and automatic doors for handicapped visitors and employees. Because four weeks have elapsed since you completed the work, we are entitled under state law to terminate our lease. This letter will serve as our 30 days' notice.

Although we have no doubt that your oversight was a good-faith error, we hope that you understand why we can't stay in the building and have made plans to go elsewhere.

We hope to remain on friendly terms during and after the move.

Sincerely,

雷諾女士，您好：

本棟大樓在四週前完成了一樓的整修作業，不知您是否未尋求法律諮詢？因為未能提供輪椅坡道和自動門供身障訪客和員工使用，您已違反《美國身心障礙者法》以及本州法律。由於自您完工後已經過四週，依本州法律，我們有權終止租約，謹以本信件作為我們的三十天提前通知。

雖然我們相信您只是一時疏忽，而非故意為之，但希望您了解為何我們無法繼續留在這棟大樓，而計畫另尋他處。

希望在我們搬離前和搬離後，都能和您維持良好的關係。

謹啟

由於寫信的目的不同，這三封信的內容也大不相同。著重於你希望引發對方做出的回應，你要的是結果。並請注意**即使在最嚴厲的版本 3 中，仍保持禮貌的口氣以促進良好關係，沒有必要充滿敵意。**

## 重點回顧

- 在開始下筆之前，想想寫作的目的和對象，據此決定內容和表達方式。
- 明白點出問題和你希望達成的結果。
- 將目標謹記於心：不要因為帶有敵意或不適當的語氣，而使效果大打折扣。

## • NOTE •

第 2 章

# 了解你的目標讀者

Understand your readers

溝通是雙向的交流，如果對於目標讀者和一般心理學一無所知，你的想法幾乎很難有效的傳達。讀者的目標和優先考量為何？他們面對什麼樣的壓力？什麼能使他們產生動力？

## 把目標讀者的時間限制納入考量

關於商業寫作目標讀者，你必須了解的重點包括：

- 你的讀者很忙，非常忙。
- 他們不認為自己有義務要讀你寫的東西。
- 如果不盡快點出重點，他們會忽略你的訊息，就像當你收到漫無重點的冗長訊息，通常也會選擇忽略。
- 若他們無法輕易理解你想表達的重點，他們便不會繼續閱讀，對你的評價也會降低。
- 如果讀者選擇跳過你的文字，那你還不如躺在床上比較省事。

隨著你在組織中的職位越高，上述這些受眾的常見行為就越明顯。因此，作為一位寫作者，你的任務是：

- 盡快證明你要說的內容不只對你重要，對讀者來說也很重要。
- 直搗重點，不浪費時間。
- 文字力求簡潔明瞭，讓讀者不僅易於閱讀，甚至樂於閱讀。
- 語氣盡量平易近人，讓讀者願意花時間在你和你的訊息上。

做到以上幾點可讓你贏得更多好感和信任，不僅可獲得實質上的競爭優勢，還可節省時間和金錢。

## 量身打造訊息內容

舉個例子，如果要寫一份給同仁們的備忘錄，你必須考量同仁在組織中的位置，以及他們可為協助組織成功做出哪些貢獻。又或者你要回覆客戶的提案要求，你必須滿足招標書上所列的每項需求，同時也必須將客戶的產業、公司規模和文化納入考量。你的語氣和內容都會隨讀者而異，你必須強調他們最關心的事物，也就是永遠的重點：「他們能獲得什麼好處（what's in it for them）」。

## 先鎖定特定讀者，再擴大目標對象

要以一大群背景各異的讀者作為寫作對象，不是一件容易的事，尤其若你根本不認識他們。但如果鎖定認識的特定對象，情況就容易得多。在美國證券交易委員會的《Plain English Handbook》這本書的序言中，巴菲特建議寫作時心中要有一個明確的讀者：

> 在寫波克夏海瑟威控股公司（Berkshire Hathaway）的年度報告時，我假裝自己是在和我的姊妹聊天。我毫不費力就能想像她們的樣子：儘管絕頂聰明，但對會計和金融卻一竅不

通。她們可以理解淺白的說法，但專業術語則會讓她們一頭霧水。我的目標很簡單：如果我們的角色互換，我會希望她們提供現在我所提供給她們的資訊。要成功做到這點，我不必有莎士比亞的文采，但我必須誠心的想與她們分享資訊。

如果你能在真正的讀者中，鎖定一個聰明但非專業人士的對象，或是和巴菲特一樣，想像自己是為家人或朋友而寫，你就能在專業深入和易於理解之間取得平衡，你的文字也會更有吸引力和說服力。

對於你要闡述的論點或分析，你的讀者可能完全沒有任何先備知識，但你可以假設他們都很聰明。只要提供他們必要的資訊，他們就能理解你講述的內容，不會被空泛虛浮的話所愚弄。

**✕ 錯誤示範：**

We aspire to be a partner primarily concerned with providing our clients the maximal acquisition of future profits and assets and focus mainly on clients with complex and multi-product needs, large and midsized corporate entities, individual or multiple entrepreneurial agents, and profit-maximizing institutional clients. By listening attentively to their needs and offering them paramount solutions, we empower those who wish to gain access to our services with the optimal set of

**○ 正確示範：**

We're a client-focused firm dedicated to making sure you get the most out of our services. Our client base includes individual entrepreneurs, midsized companies, and large corporations. If you decide to do business with us, we'll give you financial advice that is in tune with the current economy and with what you can afford to invest. For years, we've consistently received the highest possible industry ratings, and we have won the coveted Claiborne Award for exceptional client

decisions in their possible action portfolio given the economic climate at the time of the advice as well as the fiscal constraints that you are subject to. Against the backdrop of significant changes within our industry, we strive to ensure that we consistently help our clients realize their goals and thrive, and we continue to strengthen the coverage of our key clients by process-dedicated teams of senior executives who can deliver and utilize our integrated business model. On the back of a strong capital position and high levels of client satisfaction and brand recognition, we have achieved significant gains in market share. We hope that you have a favorable impression of our company's quantitative and qualitative attributes and will be inclined to utilize our services as you embark on your financial endeavors.

我們期許自己以日後為客戶取得最多利益和資產為主要目標，主要聚焦於具有複雜和多項產品需求的客戶、大型至中型企業實體、個別或多家創業代理公司，以及追求最大利潤的機構客戶。我們積極傾聽客戶需求，並提供最重要的解決方案，讓有意尋求我們服務的客

satisfaction 17 of our 37 years in business. We hope to have the opportunity to work with you in your financial endeavors.

本公司秉持客戶優先的原則，致力於確保我們的服務能為您提供最大價值。從個人創業者、中型公司到大型企業，都是我們的客戶。如果您決定與我們合作，我們會根據當前經濟情勢和你可負擔的投資金額，為您提供財務建議。多年來，我們持續榮獲業界的最高評等，在我們開業的三十七年中，共有十七年獲得業界最嚮往的克萊本獎的傑出客戶滿意獎。希望能有機會在財務規劃方面與您合作。

| ✕ 錯誤示範： | ○ 正確示範： |
| --- | --- |
| 戶，能根據提供建議時當下的經濟情勢和自身的財務限制，在可能採取的各種行動組合中，做出最佳的決策。在業界歷經劇烈變動的情況下，我們努力確保能持續協助客戶實現目標並蓬勃發展，並透過我們重視過程的高階管理人員團隊，提供及使用整合企業模型，繼續加強與主要客戶的關係。在強大資金部位以及高客戶滿意度與品牌辨識度的支援下，我們獲得了極高的市占率。希望您對我們公司質量均優的特性留下良好印象，有興趣使用我們的服務來打造您的財務規劃。 | |

## 重點回顧

- 了解讀者沒有時間可以浪費：清楚明快的直述重點，以確保訊息可確實傳達。
- 根據對象使用合適的語氣。
- 突顯對目標讀者最重要的事項。如果讀者很容易就能看出訊息與自己切身相關，他們會較有可能閱讀和回覆。
- 從目標讀者中挑選一位聰明但非專業人士的對象，或自行想像一位讀者，並根據這位特定對象來撰寫內容。如此一來，所有讀者都會覺得你的訊息更容易理解且具有說服力。

· NOTE ·

第 3 章

# 將寫作流程拆解為四個步驟

## Divide the writing process into four separate tasks

每次坐下準備寫作時是否讓你覺得備感焦慮？或許你最大的困難是不知該從何下筆。在完成收集和彙整素材之前，先別忙著想像完成後的作品。現在想像修潤後的成品還言之過早，只會讓眼前的挑戰顯得更加艱鉅。這股焦慮可能會比實際寫作耗去你更多能量。

相反的，你可以將寫作工作化整為零。不要將寫作視為一項浩大的工程，把它看作是一系列較小的步驟。

詩人、作家兼教師貝蒂蘇佛勞爾絲（Betty Sue Flowers）曾將這些步驟想像成存在於腦中的不同角色：狂人（Madman）、建築師（Architect）、木匠（Carpenter）和法官（Judge），簡稱MACJ[1]，分別代表寫作必須經歷的不同階段：

- 狂人負責收集素材和發想靈感。
- 建築師負責建立大綱，統整資訊，即使只是簡單的架構也無妨。

- 木匠負責依照建築師的規劃，將想法化為文字，串連成句子和段落。
- 法官負責為品質把關，從精簡用字到修改文法和標點符號，從頭到尾精修整篇文章。

若能大致依此順序進行，可確保以最高效率的方式產出文章。當然，這個流程可能會一再重複，例如當你發現有缺漏需要補充，你可能得回頭收集更多資料，但建議盡可能將這些步驟區分開來依序處理。

## 由狂人做開路先鋒

任何時候只要有好的靈感湧現，都應心懷感激的接受。但如果能在一開始寫作時，就有系統的進行腦力激盪，你會發現越來越多好的想法都會及早浮現。如此一來，便可大幅避免在完成並送出文件後，才終於想到絕妙的點子。

你可透過記憶、研究、觀察以及與同事和其他人的對話，甚至透過推理、猜測和想像來收集素材。你要處理的問題可能很棘手，為了找出好的解決方法讓你頭痛不已。（當財務部門的人到處駁回別人的要求，要怎麼說服他們核准你的預算申請？要如何讓執行委員會以不同的思維看待提出的合併案？）不要因為挑戰太過艱鉅而感到憂慮不

---

❶ 貝蒂蘇佛勞爾絲，〈Madman, Architect, Carpenter, Judge: Roles and the Writing Process〉，大學英語教師會議論文集 44 (1979)：7-10。

安。預先收集想法和事實可協助你過關斬將，化解對於寫作的焦慮。

初步收集到的資料要如何管理？以前，我們會用索引卡來記錄（我的前幾本書就是這樣寫出來的），但現在最簡單的方式是建立一份簡略的試算表 (spreadsheet)，並加入以下項目：

- 以標籤註明你要支持的論點。
- 針對各個論點所記下的資料、事實和意見，若要直接引述他人的話，記得要加註引號。
- 你的資料來源。引用書籍或文章時，應提供名稱和頁碼；若來源為網路，則應提供網址。（若是撰寫報告等正式文件，請參閱《The Chicago Manual of Style》了解如何正確列出參考來源。）

在作筆記時，要懂得分辨事實和意見的不同。如有必要，一定要註明出處。如果把別人的主張當成自己的意見，會讓你窒礙難行，因為你可能根本無法有說服力的支持這項論點。更糟的是，還有可能會被控抄襲。

這項基礎工作可在撰寫初稿時為你省下大把時間，還可協助建立有理有據、具說服力的文件。

## 讓建築師主導全局

一開始絞盡腦汁摸索如何組織文件時，可能會讓你感到挫折。如果做完研究和收集許多構想後，沒有合適的做法浮現腦海，你可能得再努力搜尋更多資訊。理想的狀態是能寫出三個句子，以完整的論述傳達你的觀點，接著再從讀者的角度，以最合邏輯的方式編排順序（請參閱第4章）。一般來說，這就是在開始寫初稿前，會需要的基礎大綱。

## 催促木匠在限時內完成

寫出一份理想初稿的關鍵，在於盡可能快速的寫完（第5章會有更詳細的說明）。修改校對可留待之後再做，現階段不要為了斟酌字句而拖慢速度。一旦慢下來，寫作瓶頸就會找上門來。在此階段先把法官鎖在門外，埋頭趕快寫就對了。

## 呼叫法官上場

完成整份文件後，現在可細細的琢磨如何遣辭用句、填補空缺，哪邊該加一點，哪邊該減一點。快速瀏覽文件幾次，一次檢查一個重點：引用是否正確、語氣是否恰當、轉折是否流暢等等。（如需編輯檢查清單，請見第6章。）如果想同時做好幾件事，到頭來只會一件也做不好。所以應預留充裕的時間以進行多次編輯，最起碼要預留和做研究加寫作一樣多的時間。你會發現更多的問題，也能找到更好的解決辦法。

### 重點回顧

- 著手撰寫文件時，運用MACJ法則將寫作拆解成幾個較容易處理的步驟。
- 讓狂人負責為文件收集研究和其他資料，勤於記錄引述的內容和來源。在一開始就有系統的進行腦力激盪，讓更多絕妙的想法儘早浮現。
- 建築師的工作是梳理狂人收集到的原始資料，編排成合理的大綱。將你的想法濃縮為三句主要的論述。
- 到了木匠階段，盡可能快速的寫，不必擔心文章是否完美。
- 最後，由法官負責編輯、潤飾和修改文章。分成幾個不同階段進行，一次只著重於一個寫作元素。

第 4 章

# 開始埋頭苦寫前，以完整句子記下三個主要重點

## Before writing in earnest, jot down your three main points—in complete sentences

有位數學家曾告訴我，世界上其實只有四個數字：一、二、三和其他。這麼說是有道理的：對大多數人來說，要記住四件事情似乎就是多了那麼一點。但在寫提案、報告或其他任何商業寫作時，若只有一到兩個論點支持，感覺上又有點不足。

因此，請以完整句子寫下三個主要論點，並盡可能清楚的說明你的邏輯。如此一來，你才能強迫自己徹底想清楚這麼做的理由。例如，為什麼推薦這家廠商，或為什麼向客戶提出這項建議，讓你的說明更有說服力。

如果想要邊寫邊思考架構，你會讓自己陷入麻煩，因為你還沒真正想清楚你希望讀者有怎樣的想法和反應。於是你會東拉西扯，嘗試幾次之後，才漸漸釐清想說的重點。最後，在幾經嘗試之後，你可能終於搞懂自己要說什麼，但讀者未必能跟上你的表達方式。

## 範例：如何找出重點

假設你的名字叫卡蘿桑莫，任職於一家小型管理顧問公司。你的上司史帝夫是這家公司的負責人，他想買一棟17,000平方英尺的大樓作為新辦公室。因為你是辦公室經理，因此史帝夫要你好好想想後勤規劃，並在公司提出購買大樓的出價前，寫一份你的建議。起初你很茫然，問題千頭萬緒，但你總得從某個地方著手。

因此，在開始寫備忘錄之前，你召喚腦中的狂人登場，透過腦力激盪列出需要考慮的事項：

### 腦力激盪

- Ownership 所有權
- Maintenance 維護修繕
- Buildout 裝修
- Security 安全性
- Offices vs. cubicles 辦公室vs. 小隔間
- Real-estate values — comparables? 房地產價值—同類可比資產？
- The move — bids on movers? 搬家作業—向搬家公司開價？
- Timing 時機
- Tax consequences 稅務影響
- Employee and visitor parking 員工和訪客停車位
- Environmental inspection and related issues 環境評估和相關問題
- Smooth transitioning: phone and Internet service, mail forwarding, new stationery, updating business contacts, subscriptions, etc. 順利完成過渡：電話和網路服務、郵件轉寄、新的信封信紙、更新公司聯絡資料、訂閱地址等

- Insurance 保險
- Leaving current landlord on good terms 與現任房東和平結束租約
- Taking signage to new location? 將招牌帶去新辦公室？

◆ ◆ ◆

這些只是列出主題，還沒形成完整的想法。但大致列出項目後，就可開始建築師的寫作階段，分類寫出三項要點。

## 寫出三項要點

**Steve's responsibilities (before acquisition):**

- Consider an environmental inspection to make sure that the building has no hidden issues. Our commercial realtor can help.
- Check with our accountant to find out what tax consequences we might have depending on how we time the closing.
- Ask the accountant and perhaps a tax lawyer whether Steve should own the property personally, whether the company should own it, or whether a newly formed entity (an LLC, for example) should own it. There may be liability issues.

**史帝夫的職責（購買前）：**

- 考慮進行環境評估，以確保建築沒有潛在問題。可請合作的房仲業者幫忙。
- 根據過戶交屋的時間，與會計師討論，了解會有哪些稅務影響。
- 詢問會計師或也問問稅務律師，房產應以史帝夫個人名義持有，或由公司持有，還是應該由新成立的實體（例如有限責任公司）持有。可能會有責任歸屬問題。

### My responsibilities (before acquisition):

- Cost out insurance coverage.
- Interview contractors for building out the space to our satisfaction. (Note to self: Confirm that we can roll the buildout into the mortgage.)
- Cost out the annual bill for providing the kind of security we currently have.

### 我的職責（購買前）：

- 估算保險承保範圍的成本。
- 與承包商面談，了解如何裝修空間到我們滿意。（給自己的備註：確認是否可將裝修費用納入貸款。）
- 估算若提供與目前同類型的保全系統，一年需要多少費用。

### My responsibilities (postacquisition):

- Contract for maintenance (cleaning and trash services, lawn and parking-lot care).
- Plan the move, with a smooth transition in operations (the physical move, mail forwarding, phone and Internet, new stationery, address updates, announcement to customers, moving signage, etc.).
- Help Steve plan the architectural buildout to foster collaboration and use space efficiently.

**我的職責（購買後）：**

- 簽訂維護修繕契約（打掃與垃圾清理、草坪和停車場維護）。
- 規劃搬遷事宜，確保營運順利過渡（實際搬遷作業、郵件轉寄、電話和網路、新的信封信紙、更新地址、向顧客公告、搬運招牌等）。
- 協助史帝夫規劃建築裝修，以促進同仁合作，有效運用空間。

◆ ◆ ◆

要想出以上這些內容，你必須站在史帝夫的角度，設想你會希望你的辦公室經裡考慮到哪些事項，才能協助你更好的完成工作。但這也少不了一些大量收集資訊的工作，例如若有公司最近曾搬遷或買房，可和該公司的員工聊聊。在認識的人當中，找不到這樣的人？可以請房仲業者幫忙介紹一兩位他們的客戶。

針對每個階段，我們都列出三個重要問題，或至少我們認為重要的問題。現在來看看要開始木匠的工作（寫一份實用的備忘錄給史帝夫）有多容易：

## 開始寫

**Memo**

To: Steve Haskell

From: Carol Sommers

Re: The Prospective Purchase of 1242 Maple Avenue

Date: April 10, 2025

As you requested, I've thought through the logistics of purchasing and moving into the Maple Avenue property. Here are my suggestions for each stage of the process.

收件人：史帝夫哈斯凱爾
寄件人：卡蘿桑莫
回覆：預計購買楓樹大道1242號的大樓
日期：2025年4月10日

應你所要求，我已將購買和搬遷至楓樹大道房產的後勤規劃好好想過一遍。以下是我針對各階段所提出的建議。

### Now

I'd like your approval to tackle the following tasks immediately because they'll give us a more complete picture of how expensive the acquisition and move would be:

- Cost out insurance coverage.
- Interview contractors for building out the space to our satisfaction. (I've checked with the bank to see if we can roll the buildout into the mortgage, and we can.)
- Cost out the annual bill for providing the kind of security we currently have.

### 現階段

我需要你的批准，才能立即著手處理以下事項，因為這些事項可協助我們更全盤了解購屋和搬遷所需要的費用：

- 估算保險承保範圍的成本。
- 與承包商面談，了解如何裝修空間到我們滿意。（我已經與銀行確認是否可將裝修費用納入貸款，結果是可以。）
- 估算若提供與目前同類型的保全系統，一年需多少費用。

### *Preclosing*

If you decide to go forward with the purchase and your offer is accepted, I'll take care of these items before we close on the loan:

- Arrange for at least one thorough inspection of the building.
- Work with our accountant, to the extent you'd like, to get papers in order for obtaining the bank financing you mentioned.
- Ensure that all due-diligence deadlines are met.

### *交屋前*

如果你決定購買，對方也接受你的出價，我會在完成貸款交易前處理以下事項：

- 安排至少一次徹底察看建築狀況。
- 視你需要的程度，與會計人員合作整理相關文件，以取得你提過的銀行貸款。
- 確保在期限前完成所有盡職調查。

### *After Closing*

After closing, I'll get into the nuts and bolts of the move:

- Help you plan the architectural buildout to foster collaboration and use space efficiently.
- Plan the move, with a smooth transition in operations (the physical move, mail forwarding, phone and Internet, new stationery, address updates, announcement to customers, moving signage, etc.).
- Contract for maintenance (cleaning and trash services, lawn and parking-lot care).

### 交屋後

交屋後，我就會開始處理搬遷的具體細節：

- 協助你規劃建築裝修，以促進同仁合作，有效運用空間。
- 規劃搬遷事宜，確保營運順利過渡（實際搬遷作業、郵件轉寄、電話和網路、新的信封信紙、更新地址、向顧客公告、搬運招牌等等）。
- 簽訂維護修繕契約（打掃與垃圾清理、草坪和停車場維護）。

---

### Issues for You to Think About

While I'm attending to the details above, you might want to:

- Consider environmental and structural inspections to make sure the building has no hidden issues. Our commercial realtor says he can provide guidance—I'd be happy to set up a meeting if you like.

- Check with our accountant to find out what tax consequences we might have depending on how we time the closing.
- Ask the accountant and perhaps a tax lawyer whether you should own the property personally (highly unlikely), whether Haskell Company should own it, or whether a newly formed entity (such as an LLC) should own it. You or the company may face liability issues with outright ownership.

Of course, I'm always on hand to take on whatever tasks you need. Just let me know.

### *需要你協助思考的問題*

在我處理上述細節時，或許你可以：

- 考慮進行環境和結構檢查，以確保建築沒有潛在問題。我們合作的房仲業者說可提供協助，如有需要，我可以幫忙安排見面時間。
- 根據過戶交屋的時間，與會計師討論，了解會有哪些稅務影響。
- 詢問會計師或也問問稅務律師，房產應以你的個人名義持有（可能性極低），或由哈斯凱爾公司持有，還是應該由新成立的實體（例如有限責任公司）持有。你或公司可能會有完全持有的責任歸屬問題。

當然，我會隨時準備好接手你交辦的事務，只要說一聲就行。

預先寫下三個重點，可助你寫出清楚實用的備忘錄，也有助於防止寫作瓶頸，彙整相關素材，才能提出簡潔扼要、條理清晰的建議。

但你是否注意到，這份寫好的備忘錄將重點分為四個類別，而不只三個？因為我在寫備忘錄之前，努力考慮所有細節，結果發現無法分為三類。看著初步列出的清單時，我發現少列了一段時間，而這段時間還有其他必須要做的事。因此我加上了交屋前的階段，並很快的寫下這些事項。但要是沒有一開始的計畫，我可能想不出這些項目。因為將內容彙整為三個重點，讓我能看出少了交屋前這個階段，而之後要彌補這個缺失也不至於太難。

此外，這幾個類別的順序也經過調整。為什麼將史帝夫要做的事從前面移到最後？因為這份備忘錄的重點是卡蘿桑莫，也就是身為辦公室經理的你，能為史帝夫做些什麼。為了釐清你有哪些職責，必須連史帝夫的職責也一併考慮進去。但儘管這是你最初腦力激盪的起點，備忘錄開頭可不能這麼寫。

你不能劈頭一開始就告訴你的上司他該做什麼。你沒立場這樣做，他也沒要你這樣做。所以給史帝夫的待辦事項只能放在最後，當作是個實用的提醒。這麼一來，你可以把他的注意力焦點集中在你負責的項目，讓他更容易做決定。

## 重點回顧

- 先列出要涵蓋的主題，再慢慢找出重點。
- 將這些初步想法組織成完整的句子，並分類整理出三個重點。
- 根據讀者的需求，有邏輯的將這些重點排序。

第 5 章

# 快速寫出完整內容

Write in full — rapidly

整理出三個重點並有了大方向之後，接下來就進入木匠模式，準備寫下收集和統整好的論點。盡可能快速的寫，快寫之下所寫出的句子比較簡短，用語較為自然，初稿也會在不知不覺中迅速成形。如果說寫作有什麼痛苦的地方，應該就是寫初稿的部分。因此縮短寫初稿的時間，會感覺沒那麼痛苦。

## 為自己計時

為了避免過早開始雕琢內容，你必須分秒必爭快速的寫。（創意寫作者將此稱為「限時寫作」，他們通常以此作為練習，以想出最好的點子。）規定自己必須在五到十分鐘內完成導言、正文和結語等各部分的初稿，並用電腦或手機設定計時器，以防止自己作弊。

## 不要邊寫邊校對

當木匠在工作時，法官若硬要來插一腳，只會拖慢效率。這麼做其實是一心多用，只會導致兩件事都做不好，而不是同時做好兩件事。此外，大腦中負責校對和負責生產的部分本就無法相容。誰會想要在創作新穎有趣的內容時，有個人在旁邊指手畫腳挑毛病？因此在寫初稿時，最好讓法官閃遠點，之後有的是大把時間讓你編輯。

## 不要坐等靈感從天而降

靈感很少能在你需要時降臨，但只要做好縝密的計畫，其實也不需要靠靈感。正如管理大師彼得杜拉克針對創新所說過的名言，好的寫作靠的是特意為之的精心規劃，而不是一時的「靈光乍現」。

只要遵照MACJ的寫作流程，你就是自己的靈感來源，還能大幅改善你拖拖拉拉的毛病。在狂人和建築師完成工作後，你就可著手準備開始寫作。安排好木匠該開工的時間，預定的時間一到，馬上開始動手寫。

從自己最有把握的論點開始寫起，如果中途卡住，可先跳到別的部分。總之必須維持流暢的寫作節奏。如果回頭寫當初有問題的段落時，還是難以下筆，把你想表達的想法（向自己或同事）大聲說出來。有時候用說的能幫你找到合適的字眼。重點是要先把想法訴諸文字，因為你知道下個階段還有時間可以詳細說明和潤色。

### 重點回顧

- 盡可能快速的撰寫初稿。
- 不要為了等待靈感而停滯不前。試著限定自己在五到十分鐘內完成每部分的初稿。
- 抑制自己想邊寫邊修改的衝動。將校訂留到初稿完成後再做，以防止法官出來擾亂進度。
- 安排好木匠的工作時間，時間一到馬上開始工作。
- 如果遇到障礙寫不下去，先寫其他較有把握的部分，掌握寫作節奏後，再回頭解決之前的問題。

第 6 章

# 使內容更臻完善

Improve what you've written

完成整份初稿之後，便可先修改再校對。修改是重新考量整體內容，以及文章的組織編排，是對整體架構的重新思考；校對則較傾向於對句子和段落的微調。兩者都需要時間。一方面，不要神經質的執著於追求完美，而使重要專案的進度延宕；另一方面，也不要未經妥善檢查和修改，就急忙的將文件送出。

## 修改內容

在修改文件時，問問自己幾個問題：

- 所寫內容是否完全屬實？
- 必須傳達的內容是否都已全部傳達？
- 傳達方式是否委婉公道、恰到好處？
- 文章是否具備導言、正文、結語三個部分？
- 導言部分是否開門見山、清楚具體的陳述論點？
- 是否避免了冗長的開場，明快的切入主題？

- 在正文部分，是否提出具體詳情來印證論點？
- 文章結構對閱讀者來說是否一目瞭然？標題是否提供足夠資訊？
- 結語是否呼應其他部分，但在表達上又不失新意，避免無趣的重複一樣的內容？

## 校對編輯

進入校對編輯階段，在讀這些段落字句時，要問的則是不同的問題：

- 這裡的用字可以更精簡嗎？
- 有更好的說法可表達這個想法嗎？
- 我的意思是否準確表達？
- 內容可以更有趣一點嗎？
- 表達方式是否既輕鬆又不失精確？
- 句與句之間是否前後連貫，而不顯得突兀？

## 修改和校對範例

為了更具體了解整個流程，我們來看看一則內部備忘錄如何經過三版修訂而逐漸成形。第一版初稿的內容不是很清楚，重要資訊也付之闕如，但構想已略具雛形：

## First Draft

To: All Sales Personnel
From: Chris Hedron
Subject: Changes in Order-Processing Procedure

In order to facilitate the customers' placement of orders, a new order-processing procedure has been designed. The process will require a customer to enter the product and/or service code into our order-entry system, which will then generate a quote for the job and return it to the customer for approval. This will make time for the customer to review the quote and transmit any changes before work begins. Upon receipt of the customer's written approval, the quote will be transformed into a work order. This procedure will make it easier and faster for us to process customers' orders.

收件人：所有銷售人員
寄件人：克里斯海德隆
主旨：訂單處理程序異動

為了協助客戶更輕鬆下單，我們設計了新的訂單處理程序。這個程序需要客戶在我們的訂單輸入系統輸入產品和／或服務代碼，系統便會產生工作報價並回傳給客戶，等待客戶核准。此程序可讓客戶在工作開始前，有時間可查看報價和傳送任何變更內容。只要一收到客戶的書面核准，報價就會直接轉為工單。這個程序可讓我們更輕鬆快速的處理客戶的訂單。

這份備忘錄需要再詳述更多細節，尤其是適用對象、具體做法、原因和時間等方面。第二版的初稿則較為完整，補充了很多第一版沒說清楚的部分。

## Second Draft

To: All Sales Personnel
From: Chris Hedron
Subject: New Work-Order-Processing Procedure

---

Because our current work-order-processing procedure requires a lot of paperwork and phone calls, it's difficult for customers to make changes prior to the commencement of work. The procedure is inefficient and subject to numerous errors. And it takes up to four weeks from quote to approval to work order. So we have designed a new four-step order-processing procedure that will allow customers to place orders through our website and allow us to begin jobs faster.

Beginning in January 2026, we will inform our customers about the new procedure, and on April 20, 2026, we will implement the new procedure, which will work as follows. First, to initiate or change a work order, customers can visit our website to request a quote by filling out a detailed form and providing a purchase order number. Second, we will transmit a quote to the customer for approval. Third, if the customer approves, they can return the quote with an electronic signature and purchase-order number. Fourth, we will transform the quote to a work order immediately. Work-order changes can be made using the same procedure except that instead of a quote, customers will request a work order change.

## 第二版初稿

收件人：所有銷售人員
寄件人：克里斯海德隆
主旨：新版工單處理程序

由於我們目前的工單處理程序需要大量的文書作業和電話溝通，使得客戶很難在工作開始前進行變更。這項程序效率不彰，又極容易出錯。從報價到核准到轉為工單，最長可花上四週的時間。因此，我們設計了新的四步驟工單處理程序，客戶可透過我們的網站下單，我們也可儘早開始工作。

自2026年1月開始，我們會告知客戶這項新的程序，自2026年4月20日起，新版程序就會正式上線，程序運作流程如下。首先，若要開始或變更工單，客戶可上我們的網站，填寫詳細表單並提供訂單號碼，即可要求報價。第二步，我們會將報價傳送給客戶以等待核准。第三步，若客戶核准，他們可回傳報價，並附上電子簽名和訂單號碼。第四步，我們會立即將報價轉為工單。客戶也可依相同程序變更工單，只要將要求報價改為要求變更工單即可。

此階段的重點是說明所有需要說的事項，而不是潤飾字句。接下來則可做點微調，產出更完善的版本。

## Third Draft

To: All Sales Personnel
From: Chris Hedron
Subject: New Work-Order-Processing Procedure

---

Our current work-order processing takes a lot of paperwork and phone calls, so it's hard for our customers to make changes to the work before it begins. The procedure is inefficient and subject to error. And it takes up to four weeks from quote to approval to work order. We have therefore designed a new four-step procedure that has two key benefits: (1) Customers can place orders through our website, and (2) we can start jobs faster.

Beginning January 2026, we'll tell our customers about the new procedure. On April 20, 2026 we'll implement it. The new procedure will work in four steps:

- Customers can visit our website to request a quote for a job by filling out a form and providing a purchase-order number.
- We'll then send a quote for the customer's approval.
- The customer can return the approved quote with a digital signature.
- We'll instantly convert the quote to a work order.

Work-order changes can be made using the same procedure except that instead of a quote, customers will request a work-order change.

## 第三版初稿

收件人：所有銷售人員
寄件人：克里斯海德隆
主旨：新版工單處理程序

我們目前的工單處理程序需要大量的文書作業和電話溝通，因此客戶很難在工作開始前進行變更。這項程序效率不彰，又極容易出錯。從報價到核准到轉為工單，最長可花上四週的時間。有鑑於此，我們設計了新的四步驟處理程序，此程序有以下兩大優點：(1)客戶可透過我們的網站下單，(2)我們可儘早開始工作。

自2026年1月開始，我們會告知客戶這項新的程序。在2026年4月20日，程序就會正式上線。新版程序共分為四個步驟：

- 客戶可上我們的網站，填寫表單並提供訂單號碼，即可要求工作報價。
- 我們會傳送報價以等待客戶核准。
- 客戶可回傳核准的報價，並附上電子簽名。
- 我們會立即將報價轉換為工單。

客戶也可依相同程序變更工單，只要將要求報價改為要求變更工單即可。

### 重點回顧

- 預留充裕的修改和校訂時間。
- 從整體上審視你的初稿，以新的角度檢視內容和架構：要傳達的事項是否都已透過最有效的方式傳達？
- 接著便可編輯微調，讓文章更簡練、清晰和精確。

· NOTE ·

第7章

# 善用圖表來闡述和說明

## Use graphics to illustrate and clarify

如果要闡述較複雜的概念，或想要有效的調整一長串文字的架構，像這種時候，一份簡潔的圖表可讓你一目瞭然的呈現重要資訊。對於想快速瀏覽重點的讀者來說，使用這類圖表特別能投其所好。

但有幾項重要原則必須注意：

- 確保圖表呼應文字所討論的內容。
- 將圖表置於說明的文字附近，最好在同一頁，或放在相對頁。
- 使用讀者可輕鬆理解的圖例和符號。

若要了解如何製作有效的圖表，請參閱Edward Tufte的著作，尤其是《Envisioning Information》和《Beautiful Evidence》。這些超強視覺輔助圖表背後的學問和深思熟慮，會讓你讚嘆不已。

說到這，如果不放個圖表就結束，實在是說不過去，因此就以下表來為本章作結。你會發現當你快速翻過本書時，你的目光會在這頁停留，這是因為偏離常態的東西可達到特別強調的效果。假如每三到四頁就放個圖表，就無法達到相同效果。所以要讓圖表顯得獨特，而不要過度濫用。

| | |
|---|---|
| **Who**<br>誰是你的目標對象？ | 重點 考慮目標讀者的考量、動機和背景。 |
| **Why**<br>你的寫作原因為何？ | 重點 牢記你寫作的目的，每個句子都應朝著這個目標前進。 |
| **What**<br>須傳達的內容為何？ | 重點 只納入有助於傳達訊息的重點和細節。 |
| **When**<br>何時應執行動作？ | 重點 說明時間安排。 |
| **How**<br>如何向讀者說明好處？ | 重點 向讀者明確說明你會如何滿足他們的需求。 |

## 重點回顧

- 將報告內容（或部分內容）濃縮為圖表、圖解或其他視覺輔助素材，協助目標對象了解內容和其重要性。
- 參考你覺得有效的視覺素材來設計你的圖表。
- 參閱 Edward Tufte 的著作以培養圖表製作技能。

- Section -

# 2

# 培養寫作能力

## Developing Your Skills

第 8 章

# 不厭其煩的清楚說明

Be relentlessly clear

把話說得清楚明白就像把雙面刃。當你直率的表明立場或建議採取某個做法，這是在冒很大的風險。因此，不想承擔風險的人會將內容寫得含糊不清。或許他們是想保留模糊空間，好隨事態發展見風使舵；又或者他們是想在之後進展順利時邀功，在搞砸時推諉責任。

但事實上，多數讀者不會覺得這種人是見機行事的識時務者，只會認為他們沒骨氣、人云亦云，無法快速看準眼前的機會（更遑論抓住機會）。因此，寫作時應避免含糊籠統。

## 站在讀者的角度

判斷是否夠清楚時，理應從讀者的角度判斷，而不是你的角度。可試試將初稿拿給沒看過的同事過目，請他們指出你要表達的重點為何。如果他們無法正確指出，就表示你的表達不夠清楚。

寫作的理想狀態應該是意思不容錯認，確保讀者沒有誤會或曲解的空間。任何需要讀者花多餘心力理解的內容，都會讓他們無法全心專注閱讀，最終難免會產生誤解。

## 保持用詞簡潔

行文簡潔，意思自然清楚明白。盡可能多用簡短的字句。這些年來，研究已一再證實，最適合閱讀的理想句子長度，是平均不超過二十個字。你可能需要來點變化，用些極短或極長的句子來抓住讀者的興趣，但應以平均二十個字為目標。對每一個句子，都問問自己是否還能再更簡短。

| ✕ 錯誤示範： | ○ 正確示範： |
| --- | --- |
| Efficiency measures that have been implemented by the company with strong involvement of senior management have generated cost savings while at the very same time assisting in the building of a culture that is centered around the value of efficiency. We anticipate that, given this excising of unnecessary expenditures and enhanced control of other expenditures, the overall profitability of the company will be increased in the near term of up to four quarters.<br><br>公司所實行的提升效率措施和高階管理人員的強勢介入，不僅節省了成本，同時也協助建立了重視效率的文化。我們預期只要刪除不必要的支出，並加強控制其他花費，公司近期的整體獲利率可望在四個季度內有所提升。 | Our senior management team has cut costs and made the company more efficient. We expect to be more profitable for the next four quarters.<br><br>我們的高階管理團隊已降低成本，提高公司效率，期望在未來四個季度可獲得更高的利潤。 |

如果要為非專業人士的讀者撰寫較專門的主題，例如向使用者說明軟體升級的好處，或是為公司參加401(k) 退休計畫的同仁彙整投資入門指南，別在專業術語第一次出現時，就急著提供定義。這樣會使句子變得冗長，讓讀者更難理解意思。有時你可能得重新起個句子，或甚至新的段落，用淺顯易懂的英文來解釋一個術語或概念。

## 具體呈現，不要空洞描述

你在學校的寫作課可能曾聽老師說過：「要具體呈現，不要只是空洞描述。」（Show, don't tell.）這對撰寫任何形式的內容，即便是商業文件，都是極好的建議。這句話的重點在於要具體呈現細節，引導讀者自行得出結論（當然，他們的結論必須與你的相同），而不是只陳述你的意見，沒有任何論點支持，就想讓讀者買帳。

試想想以下範例：

| ✕ 錯誤示範： | ○ 正確示範： |
| --- | --- |
| He was a bad boss.<br>他是個壞上司。 | He got a promotion based on his assistant's detailed reports, but then—despite the company's record profits—denied that assistant even routine cost-of-living raises.<br>他靠著助理詳盡的報告而獲得升遷，但儘管公司獲利創下新高，他卻連給助理因應生活物價上漲的例行加薪都拒絕。 |

| ✕ 錯誤示範： | ○ 正確示範： |
| --- | --- |
| The company lost its focus and floundered.<br><br>這間公司已失去焦點而陷入困境。 | The CEO acquired five unrelated subsidiaries — as far afield as a paper company and a retailer of children's toys — and then couldn't service the $26 million in debt.<br><br>執行長併購了五間子公司，包括一家紙業公司和一家兒童玩具零售商，子公司彼此的業務天差地遠、毫不相關，致使公司無法償還兩千六百萬的債務。 |
| The shares of OJM stock issued to Pantheon stockholders in the merger will constitute a significant proportion of the outstanding stock of OJM after the merger. Based on this significant proportion, it is expected that OJM will issue millions of OJM shares to Pantheon stock holders in the merger.<br><br>在合併案後，因合併案而發給Pantheon股東的OJM股份，會在OJM的流通股中佔有相當大的比例。根據這個極大的比例，預計OJM將會在合併案中發放數百萬OJM股份給Pantheon的股東。 | We expect that OJM will issue about 320 million shares of its stock to Pantheon shareholders in the merger. That figure will account for about 42% of OJM's outstanding stock after the merger.<br><br>我們預期OJM會在這次合併案中，發放大約三億兩千萬的股份給Pantheon的股東。在合併案後，這個數字在OJM的流通股中約佔42%的比例。 |

## 透過寫信來磨練技能

從一個人寫的信，最能看出整體寫作技能的指標。同時，寫信也是最安全的練習方式，可為撰寫更困難的內容形式預做準備。可撰寫的信件類型從感謝函、祝賀信、推薦信（如有人要求）、投訴信，到寫給編輯的信和私人信件（手寫），林林總總，不一而足。如果能把信寫好，幾乎寫什麼都難不倒你（參見第19章，了解如何撰寫「商業信件」），因為寫信可幫助你把焦點放在讀者身上。在寫信時，你是在與一位特定的收信人聯絡溝通，並可透過信件與對方建立良好關係。電子郵件或許可讓對方留下印象，但遠不及私人手寫信來得令人記憶深刻。

為了培養寫信習慣，你可試著每週寫幾封信，其中最好包含多份手寫信件。（當你在一疊郵件中收到一封手寫信，這封信不會第一時間吸引你的注意嗎？）這類信件較為私人，若寫得好，更有值得留念或甚至保存的價值，是與他人建立或維繫關係的一大助力。透過寫信告訴你的下屬，你有多感謝他們的努力，或恭喜同事升遷，激勵團隊成員達成目標，也可告訴新的合作夥伴，你很期待與他們共事。要寫好一封信，字跡要工整，盡量不超過一頁，保持親切友善的語氣，多提對方少提自己，並使用成熟、有品味的信紙。

一句簡短籠統的句子（例如He was a bad boss.「他是個壞上司」）或許會在讀者腦中留下印象，但只會被認為是可能帶有偏見的個人觀感；除非說話的人非常可信，這句話才會顯得可信。至於關於OJM股票那句又長又含糊的句子，讀者根本沒有著力點，只會疲於嘗試閱讀。

具體的商業寫作之所以有說服力，原因就在於有根據、有條理以及有記憶點。當你提供客觀、有意義的詳細說明（例如，說明陷入困境的公司couldn't service the $26 million in debt「無法償還兩千六百萬的債務」），這是在分享資訊，而不只是聲稱公司lost its focus「已失去焦點」的個人看法。表現出掌握事實的能力，可讓你更具有公信力，你的訊息也能更禁得起時間考驗。與具體細節相比，一般人根本不在乎或甚至不記得抽象空泛的內容。

因此，假設你要向潛在客戶推銷公司的諮詢服務，別只是說能幫他們省錢，說說你幫其他人省了多少錢；別光保證能讓他們的生活更輕鬆省事，列舉你能幫他們處理哪些耗時的事；別淨說自己與醫療保健業合作的經驗豐富，列出具體對象，說說曾與哪幾家醫院和醫學中心合作。此外，還要附上客戶的見證，說他們有多滿意你為他們省下的時間和金錢。

## 重點回顧

- 從讀者的角度評估自己的表達是否夠清楚。最好能請同事快速看過一遍初稿，看看他們是否能正確總結出重點。
- 盡可能使用簡潔明瞭的措詞，以每個句子平均不超過二十字為目標。
- 提供具體細節讓讀者了解，而非以空泛的宣稱就想試圖讓他們信服。
- 培養寫信的能力，以提升各方面的寫作技能。

第9章

# 了解如何正確撰寫摘要

Learn to summarize—accurately

一篇好的摘要應該要具體明確，並擺在文件的開頭，讓讀者不用費心尋找。好的摘要會直陳重點，為整篇內容奠定基礎，對重要資訊毫無保留的分享。

以下是兩份建議回絕某份提案的文件開頭，看看這兩者有何不同：

**✕ 錯誤示範：**

Summary
The cell phone changeover that has been proposed should be rejected. For the reasons stated below, the company would not be well served by accepting the proposal.

摘要
應該拒絕轉換電信業者的提案。基於以下所述原因，接受這項提案並不會讓公司獲得更好的服務。

## ○ 正確示範：

Summary

Last year, we adopted an officewide policy of issuing cell phones to all executives and sales reps at an annual cost of $58,000 (including voice and data plans). The Persephone company has proposed that we switch to its phones and service at an annual cost of $37,000. The committee charged with evaluating this proposal recommends that we reject it for four reasons:

1. The new plans would have significantly less coverage in Europe and Asia, so our international sales reps might suffer lost opportunities.
2. Our current provider has been highly responsive and has tailored its service to our needs.
3. The $21,000 savings is dwarfed by potential costs (even one dropped sales call could result in a loss of much more money than that).
4. Persephone's customer service appears from credible online reviews to be inferior.

摘要

去年，我們在全公司內部施行了一項政策，配給每位高階主管和銷售代表一部手機，一年的費用為$58,000美元（含通話和資費方案）。Persephone公司提出了一項方案，若改用他們的手機和服務，一年的費用為$37,000美元。負責評估此提案的委員會基於以下四個原因，建議拒絕此提案：

1. 新資費方案所涵蓋的範圍在歐洲和亞洲地區大幅減少，我們的跨國銷售代表可能會因此錯失商機。

2. 我們目前合作的服務供應商回覆問題非常積極，並針對我們的需求，量身打造服務項目。
3. 與可能付出的代價相比，省下$21,000美元根本微不足道（即使只漏接一通銷售電話，損失的金額都可能遠勝於此）。
4. 根據可靠的網路評論，Persephone公司的顧客服務似乎較為遜色。

---

第二個版本較好的原因為何？第二版好在**無論任何人在任何時候讀這段摘要，都能完全了解內容。**相較之下，第一版則假設讀者已熟知情況，因此只有少數「內部人士」才能明白，且僅限於特定期間。此外，由於內容含糊不清，也無法像第二版因提供具體說明而顯得有公信力。

抓不準該提供多少細節，才能恰到好處寫出清楚實用的摘要嗎？你可以根據文件內容，寫一份描述性的大綱。用一句話為每個段落做總結，記錄何人（Who）、何事（What）、何時（When）、何地（Where）、為何（Why）及如何（How）等要素，試著以此為脈絡來完成整份摘要。同時，以讀者的需求為最優先的考量。當讀者打開文件時，他們會有什麼問題？針對這些問題，提供簡短但具體的回答，向讀者保證接下來的內容對他們很重要。

## 要簡短，但也不能太短

一般人常認為摘要應該要越短越好，但若內容空洞，即使寫得簡短也毫無價值。說得太多固然不好，但說得太少，也一樣不適當。應站在讀者的觀點，為了讓他們了解最新情況，盡可能提供必要資訊。你可以把摘要想成像CliffsNotes學習指南提供的濃縮版一樣。上面第二個範例的內容雖然較長，但它完整傳達了訊息要點，全文沒有一個贅字，這正是下一章要講的重點。

## 重點回顧

- 在文件一開頭便總結重要資訊。
- 用一句話為每個段落作結，說明5W1H（Who、What、When、Where、Why和How），用這些句子建構出完整摘要。
- 只提供讀者了解問題所需的資訊，不要太多，也不要太少。

# 第 10 章

# 拒絕贅字

## Waste no words

用字應力求精簡。如果能用before表達，就不要用prior to，更不要用prior to the time when。

雖然prior to是可在字典上查到的用字選擇，但並非好的選擇。一個字能說清楚，就不要用兩個字；兩個字能說清楚，就不用三個字。當字數快速增加，讀者的理解速度則會變慢。當然，還是得顧及英語的慣用語法。在該加冠詞（a、an、the）的地方，別擅自將其刪去。也別老是省略that這個重要的字，大多數時候，必須有that意思才清楚。該刪去的是那些沒有實質功能的字，刪除贅字可節省讀者的時間和心力，讓你的想法更容易傳達及應用。

冗詞贅字可能出現在許多不同情況，從雜亂無章的陳述，到毫無必要的重複，或是有更簡短精準的文字可取代的冗長用詞。無論是何種形式的贅字，都不是件好事。試想想以下範例：

| ✕ 錯誤示範： | ○ 正確示範： |
| --- | --- |
| The trend in the industry is toward self-generation by some companies of their own websites, and Internet technology is changing the nature of training necessary to acquire the skill of website development at an acceptable level of sophistication, so that this activity can more and more be handled in-house.<br><br>[49字]<br><br>業界趨勢是傾向由某些公司自行研發網站，網路技術也改變了在可接受的複雜度上，學習網站開發技能所需的訓練本質，因此有越來越多公司可交由內部人員研發網站。 | Since Internet technology makes it easier than ever to develop sophisticated web sites, some companies now develop their own in-house.<br><br>[19字]<br><br>由於網路技術讓開發複雜的網站變得前所未有的簡單，現在有些公司都可由內部人員自行研發網站。 |
| We are unable to fill your order at this point in time because there is an ongoing dock strike that affects our operations.<br><br>[23字]<br><br>因為正在進行的港口罷工影響了我們的營運，此時我們沒有辦法履行你的訂單。 | We cannot fill your order right now because of the dock strike.<br><br>[12字]<br><br>由於港口罷工，我們目前無法履行你的訂單。 |
| I am writing in response to a number of issues that have arisen with regard to the recent announcement that there will be an increase in the charge for the | You may have heard that we're raising the fees for using our lobby computers.<br><br>[14字] |

| ✕ 錯誤示範： | ○ 正確示範： |
| --- | --- |
| use of our lobby computers.<br>[35字]<br>我寫這封信是為了回應因為近期一項公告而引發的許多問題，該公告表示使用休息室電腦的費用即將調漲。 | 你可能已經聽說，我們調漲了休息室電腦的使用費用。 |
| The greater number of these problems can readily be dealt with in such a way as to bring about satisfactory solutions.<br>[21字]<br>這些問題中，絕大部分都可透過令人滿意的解決方案輕鬆處理。 | Most of these problems can be readily solved.<br>[8字]<br>這些問題大部分都可輕鬆解決。 |

若要刪減文件中的贅字，可試試以下訣竅：

- **將所有可刪除的介系詞刪除**，尤其是of：將April of 2025改為April 2025，將point of view改為viewpoint。
- **如果可以，將所有以 -ion結尾的名詞改為動詞**，例如將was in violation of改為violated，將provided protection to改為protected。
- 盡可能**將*is*、*are*、*was*和*were*以較有力的動詞取代**。將was hanging改為hung，將is indicative of改為indicates。

以下是運用上述三個訣竅的範例：

| ✕ 錯誤示範： | ○ 正確示範： |
| --- | --- |
| The manufacturers of tools for gardening have been the victims of a compression factor that has resulted in an increase in units on the market accompanied by a negative disproportionate rise of prices.<br>[36字]<br>因為某種壓縮因素導致市場上工具數量增加，加上不成比例的價格上漲，使得園藝工具的製造商深受其害。 | The garden-tool industry has suffered from an oversupply of units coupled with rising prices.<br>[14字]<br>園藝工具產業因為供過於求和價格上漲而大受打擊。 |
| For the near and intermediate future in terms of growth goals, Bromodrotics, Inc., is evaluating its corporate design needs. The purpose of this short-term and intermediate-term evaluation is to make a determination as to how the image of the company might best be positioned to be of assistance to the sales force in meeting its growth goals.<br>[57字]<br>Bormodrotics, Inc.正在就近期和中期的成長目標評估公司的設計需求。短期和中期評估的目的，是為了決定公司形象的最佳定位，以協助提升銷量，達成成長目標。 | To increase sales, Bromodrotics needs to improve its image.<br>[9字]<br>若要提高銷量，Bormodrotics必須提升公司形象。 |

請儘管大刀闊斧的刪減初稿字數，只要注意不違反英文自然道地的聲音和節奏即可。注意別為了壓縮字數，而使內容聽來過於簡略不自然。

上述最後一例所用的另一個訣竅是刪除像in terms of和the purpose of等多餘的詞彙。有時候，你甚至會看到以下更冗贅的用語：

in this connection it might be observed that 從這個情形可看出

it is important to bear in mind that 務必切記

it is interesting that 有趣的是

it is notable that 值得注意的是

it is worthwhile to note that 值得留意的是

it should be pointed out that 需要指出的是

it will be remembered that 會被眾人記住的是

這些詞還是少用為妙，更不用說 it goes without saying that...（顯而易見的⋯）。

## 重點回顧

- 不說多餘的廢話：在能保持用詞自然的前提下，能用兩個字說明的，就不要用到三個字。
- 若要精簡文章內容，可刪去不必要的介系詞，盡可能以動作動詞取代抽象的-ion名詞，並以更簡單直接的動詞取代囉嗦的be動詞片語。
- 刪除沒有實質意義的贅詞。

## • NOTE •

第 11 章

# 用字簡單直接：避免商務用語

## Be plain-spoken: Avoid bizspeak

無論你是想成為跳脫傳統思維（outside-the-box thinking）的佼佼者（best-of-breed），或單純想激勵（incentivize）同仁在核心職能（core-performance）的附加價值（value-adds）上達到典範轉移（paradigm shift），淺顯直白的表達是必不可少的關鍵任務（mission-critical）。以最具創新性（leading-edge）的方式運用（leverage）直白用語的綜合技能（skill set），可確保你的可執行（actionable）項目可為你與時俱進（future-proof）的資產和包含所有知識的儲存庫（global-knowledge repository）帶來加乘作用（synergize）。

以上這段純屬玩笑，但說真的，簡單清晰的表達真的很重要。我們都想聽起來像個人在說話，而不是像機構的宣傳。不過知易行難，尤其若身邊的同事都愛秀兩句流行術語，正因如此，我們才需要練習。

在以前記者用字比現今講究的時代，報社編輯通常都有一份「禁用字目錄」，列出在任何情況下都不該出現在報紙上的字詞（但若為引述內容則屬例外情況）。以下也有一份商業寫作應避免的詞彙。當然，這只是個起點，遇到其他妨礙溝通的商務用語時，你也可將該用語加入這份清單，用實質的想法來取代這些過度濫用的詞句。

## 商業用語黑名單

| 用語 | 字義 |
| --- | --- |
| actionable | 可執行的（意指法律訴訟時不在此限） |
| agreeance | 協議 |
| as per | 根據 |
| at the end of the day | 最後 |
| back of the envelope | 粗略估算 |
| bandwidth | 精力、資源（非指電子產品的頻寬） |
| bring our A game | 全力以赴 |
| client-centered | 以客為尊 |
| come-to-Jesus | 關鍵時刻 |
| core competency | 核心職能 |
| CYA | 保障自己 |
| drill down | 深入探究 |
| ducks in a row | 有條不紊 |
| forward initiative | 前瞻性倡議 |
| going forward | 從今以後 |
| go rogue | 失控 |
| guesstimate | 粗略估算 |
| harvesting efficiencies | 收穫效益 |
| hit the ground running | 立即行動 |

| | |
|---|---|
| impact | 影響（用作動詞） |
| incent | 鼓勵 |
| incentivize | 激勵 |
| impactful | 有影響力的 |
| kick the can down the road | 往後推遲 |
| Let's do lunch. | 一起吃午餐。 |
| Let's take this offline. | 私下再談。 |
| level the playing field | 打造公平競爭環境 |
| leverage | 運用（用作動詞） |
| liaise | 聯繫 |
| mission-critical | 重要任務 |
| monetize | 營利 |
| net-net | 總結來說 |
| on the same page | 達成共識 |
| operationalize | 落實 |
| optimize | 最佳化 |
| out of pocket | 缺席（意指費用時不在此限） |
| paradigm shift | 典範轉移 |
| parameters | 參數 |
| per | 按照 |
| planful | 計畫周詳的 |
| pursuant to | 根據 |
| push the envelope | 挑戰極限 |
| putting lipstick on a pig | 想美化缺點卻徒勞無功 |
| recontextualize | 重新詮釋 |

| | |
|---|---|
| repurpose | 重新利用 |
| rightsized | 精簡規模 |
| sacred cow | 神聖不可侵犯的事物 |
| scalable | 可擴充的 |
| seamless integration | 無縫整合 |
| seismic shift | 重大變化（非指地震） |
| smartsized | 調整規模 |
| strategic alliance | 策略聯盟 |
| strategic dynamism | 動態調整策略 |
| synergize; synergy | 加乘；加乘作用 |
| think outside the box | 跳脫傳統思維 |
| throw it against the wall and see if it sticks | 嘗試看看是否有效 |
| throw under the bus | 為個人利益犧牲他人 |
| turnkey | 統包專案 |
| under the radar | 保持低調 |
| utilization; utilize | 使用率；使用 |
| value-added | 附加價值 |
| verbage | 贅詞（正確的拼法為 verbiage，僅限於指冗長的措辭） |
| where the rubber meets the road | 見真章的時刻 |
| win-win | 雙贏 |

以上都是已在商務領域蔚為風潮的詞句，建議你能不用就盡量不用。有時候，人們使用這些詞句，是為了提升歸屬感，或為了聽起來「很內行」。也或許在他們的觀念裡，好的寫作就是要非常正式，所

以當他們一打起字或拿起筆，整個人就生硬起來，堆疊出通篇的陳腔濫調。

要讓寫作風格達到和口說一樣的程度，需要經驗的累積，以及用心地修改，修到看不出曾修改的程度。

| ✕ 錯誤示範： | ○ 正確示範： |
| --- | --- |
| The reduction in monthly assessments which will occur beginning next month has been made financially feasible ***as a result of leveraging*** our substantial reductions in expenditures.<br>為了有效大幅縮減開支，在財務方面，刪減每月評估費用將自下個月開始實施。 | We'll be cutting your assessments beginning next month because we've saved on expenses.<br>為了節省開支，我們將自下個月起刪減評估費用。 |
| ***It is to be noted that*** a considerable amount of savings has been made possible ***by reason of our planful initiation of*** more efficient and effective purchasing procedures.<br>在有計畫的採用更有效率和成效的採購程序後，我們發現成功的省下了相當大筆的經費。 | We've saved considerable sums by streamlining our purchases.<br>精簡採購程序讓我們省下了大筆經費。 |

## 找出令人不快的用詞

開始留意在各種文件中出現的商務用語，你會發現從備忘錄到行銷計畫，這些用語無所不在。最後，你就能在自己的寫作中揪出這些用詞，並加以避免。你會學會避開像 Attached please find 這樣的制式用語，以及其他只會讓訊息更顯雜亂的詞彙。

乍看之下，商務用語似乎是簡便的表達方式，但在讀者眼裡，你只是無意識的使用他們已經聽膩的公式化用語。相形之下，簡短易讀的文件，才能顯現出在乎和體貼。Attached please find 只是眾多錯誤示範中的一例：

| ✕ 錯誤示範： | ○ 正確示範： |
| --- | --- |
| at your earliest convenience<br>在你方便時儘早 | as soon as you can<br>盡快 |
| in light of the fact that<br>鑒於此一事實 | because<br>因為 |
| we are in receipt of<br>我們已收到 | we've received<br>我們已收到 |
| as per our telephone conversation on today's date<br>就我們今天電話中所討論的內容 | as we discussed this morning<br>就我們今早討論的內容 |
| Pursuant to your instructions, I met with Roger Smith today regarding the above-mentioned.<br>儘管以上所提之事，我今天還是依照你的指示與羅傑史密斯碰面了。 | As you asked, I met with Roger Smith today.<br>依你的要求，我今天與羅傑史密斯碰面了。 |

| ✕ 錯誤示範： | ○ 正確示範： |
| --- | --- |
| Please be advised that the deadline for the above mentioned competition is Wednesday, April 2, 2025.<br>請注意，上述所提競賽的截止日期是2025年4月2日星期三。 | The deadline is April 2, 2025.<br>截止日期是2025年4月2日。 |
| Thank you for your courtesy and cooperation regarding this matter.<br>感謝你對此事的關照與配合。 | Thank you.<br>謝謝。 |
| Thank you in advance for your courtesy and cooperation in this regard. Please do not hesitate to contact me if you have any questions regarding this request.<br>對於你對此事的關照與配合，在此先行致謝。若對此要求有任何問題，歡迎隨時與我聯絡。 | Thank you. If you have any questions, please call.<br>謝謝。如有任何問題，歡迎來電。 |

清晰明瞭的寫作風格，是指在顧及語意和語氣的同時，盡可能直截了當的表達想法。

讓我們再次以巴菲特為例，他除了是世界上最聰明的企業領導人之一，對於商業寫作的好壞他也非常注重。看看他是如何改寫一家金融服務公司企業簡介中的一個段落。先讀過第一份摘錄內容，再讀下方巴菲特改寫的版本，注意那些經過他精簡改寫後被刪掉的商務詞彙：

## ✕ 錯誤示範：

Maturity and duration management decisions are made ***in the context of*** an intermediate maturity orientation. The maturity structure of the portfolio is adjusted ***in the anticipation of*** cyclical interest-rate changes. Such adjustments are not made ***in an effort to*** capture short-term, day-to-day movements in the market, but instead ***are implemented in anticipation of*** longer-term, secular shifts in the interest rates (i.e., shifts transcending and/or not inherent to the business cycle). Adjustments made to shorten portfolio maturity and duration are made to limit capital losses during periods when interest rates are expected to rise. Conversely, adjustments made to lengthen maturation for the portfolio's maturity and duration strategy lies ***in the analysis of*** the U.S. and global economies, focusing on levels of real interest rates, monetary and fiscal policy actions, and cyclical indicators.

到期期限和存續期間的管理決策，是以中期到期期限傾向為依據。投資組合的到期期限結構，會依預測的週期利率變化進行調整。我們不會因為市場上的每日短期波動來改變期限，而是隨著長期利率走向的預測來做調整（也就是說，是超越和／或不受景氣循環影響的變動）。調整以縮短投資組合到期期限和存續期間，是為了在預測升息時限制資金損失。相反的，調整延長投資組合到期期限和存續期間的策略，則是基於美國和全球經濟情勢的分析，著重於實際利率水準、貨幣和財務政策執行，以及循環週期指標。

字數：136

句數：5（全為被動語態）

平均每句長度：27.2字

易讀性指數：8.2

### ○ 正確示範：

We will try to profit by correctly predicting future interest rates. When we have no strong opinion, we will generally hold intermediate-term bonds. But when we expect a major and sustained increase in rates, we will concentrate on short-term issues. And conversely, if we expect a major shift to lower rates, we will buy long bonds. We will focus on the big picture and won't make moves based on short-term considerations.

我們的獲利方式是靠準確預測未來的利率走向。如果沒有明確的看法，我們一般會持有中期債券。但若預期利率會有較大的長期漲幅，則會著重於短期債券發行。相反的，若預期主要走向為降息，我們便會購入長期債券。我們注重的是整體形勢，不會因為短期的考量而妄動。

字數：74
句數：5（沒有被動語態）
平均每句長度：14.8字
易讀性指數：60.1

「弗雷奇易讀性指數」（Flesch Reading Ease，FRE）是由研究易讀性的專家魯道夫弗雷奇（Rudolf Flesch）所研發的一項檢測工具，可根據字數和句子長度衡量一段文字是否易於理解。如果用這項指數來分析修改前和修改後的簡介內容，就可以將兩者的差異量化。分數越高，表示文字越容易閱讀和理解。從0到100的級距中，上方原本136字的簡介得到8.2分。相較之下，下方巴菲特改寫的版本則獲得60.1分。為了讓你有些概念，《讀者文摘》的易讀性指數是65，《時代雜誌》大約是52，《哈佛法律評論》則是30出頭。提高文字的易讀性不等於「簡化內容」。上例中修改後的段落仍提供讀者相同的資訊，但整體表達清楚得多。

以下是一個較短的範例，節錄自一間社區大學的成立宗旨：

**✕ 錯誤示範：**

The object of this enterprise is ***to facilitate the development of greater capacities*** for community colleges and not-for-profit neighborhood organizations to ***engage in heightened collaboration in regard to the provision of*** community services that would maximize the available resources from a number of community stakeholders and to ***provide a greater level of*** communication about local prioritization of educational needs with the particular community.
[63字]

本計畫的宗旨為協助社區大學和社區的非營利組織發展更大的潛力，在提供社區服務方面加強合作，從眾多參與社區事務的人員獲取最多可用資源，並對當地該特定社區教育需求的優先順序，提供更高的溝通層級。

**○ 正確示範：**

This project seeks to help community colleges and nonprofit neighborhood groups work more efficiently together.
[15字]

本計畫是為了協助社區大學和社區的非營利組織更有效率的合作。

---

在巴菲特和社區大學這兩個例子中，原始版本似乎都無意把重點說清楚。原作者可能是想讓自己聽起來很厲害，或是想掩飾真正的目的，又或者是想掩蓋他們也不全然知道自己的目的是什麼。無論答案為何，對任何目標讀者來說，原本的寫作風格都無法發揮作用。

**重點回顧**

- 以達到和口說一樣自然的寫作為目標：以人的角度下筆，而非公司或組織。
- 避免公式化的用語，這些用語會讓內容顯得死氣沉沉，顯示出你懶得思考。
- 盡可能直接的表達想法，以提高易讀性。

## • NOTE •

第 12 章

# 依先後順序陳述事情經過

## Use chronology when giving a factual account

故事的本質就是依時間順序記敘，按事情發生的先後，一件件交代。這樣的結構不僅適用於書籍和電影，在商業寫作上也一樣管用。這種敘事方式較可能清楚、有效率的表達，讓讀者有興趣讀下去。因此，就如老電視影集《警網》的主角喬富萊帝常說的那句話，「女士，只要陳述事實就好」。只要依正確的順序，陳述重要的事實。

理論上，這點似乎顯而易見，但實際上，說好一個故事對寫作者來說並不容易。他們經常沒有交代原委，就自顧自講述起來，結果讀者當然看得一頭霧水。你對以下情況應該不陌生，我們與家人朋友常會有這樣的對話：「等等，重來一遍，這是什麼時候的事？你當時在哪？你為什麼會跟這個人說話？他是從哪冒出來的？」

假設你要寄一封電子郵件說明目前專案的進度，而距離上一次討論此事已經有一段時間。收件人參與這個專案的程度沒有你深，且手邊可能有其他許多事情在忙。因此，你應該先回顧上次提到這個主題時的情況，再說明自那之後的發展：

**✕ 錯誤示範：**

Sarah—

It was hard making headway with Jim Martinez, but finally we're looking (in the best-case scenario) at a demonstration of what our software can do by mid-May, as I established in my first telephone conference with Jim last Monday at 9:00 a.m. He was out Wednesday and Thursday (I didn't see any reason to try calling on Tuesday), but on Friday he told me that we'd need a sample app. But prior to that, Magnabilify requires an NDA. Tuesday's meeting should clarify things. Let me know what you think.

Frank

莎拉：

要與吉姆馬丁尼茲聯絡上真不容易，但我們終於敲定（理想情況下）在五月中之前展示我們軟體的功能，因為我在上週一早上九點和吉姆進行了第一次電話會議。他上週三和週四都不在（而我看不出必須在週二致電的理由），但週五他說我們必須提供應用程式樣本。不過在那之前，Magnabilify 要我們先簽保密協議。下週二的面談應該會釐清相關細節。讓我知道你有什麼想法。

**○ 正確示範：**

Sarah—

Last week you asked me to approach Magnabilify Corporation, the software developers, to see whether they might have any interest in our customizing some security applications for their computer systems. I finally got through to Jim Martinez, corporate vice president in charge of software, and we have planned a face-to-face meeting at his office next Tuesday.
The next steps, as I understand them under Magnabilify's protocol, will be to enter into a nondisclosure agreement, to develop a sample application (in less than two weeks), and to schedule a demonstration shortly after.
Can you and I chat before Tuesday's meeting?

Frank

莎拉：

上週你要我與軟體開發商 Magnabilify 公司接洽，看看他們是否有興趣由我們為他們的電腦系統客製化一些安全應用程式。我終於與他們負責軟體業務的的副總裁吉姆馬丁尼茲聯絡上，並約好下週二在他的辦公室面談。

| ✕ 錯誤示範： | ○ 正確示範： |
|---|---|
| 法蘭克 | 根據我從 Magnabilify 的規程對他們的了解，接下來的流程包括簽訂保密協議、開發應用程式樣本（兩週內），以及盡快安排演示時間。<br>在下週二的面談之前，你能先和我談談嗎？<br>法蘭克 |

左邊的版本像是意識流的寫法。寫作者未能退一步從讀者的角度思考，然後依先後次序將重點娓娓道來。即使是像右邊版本這樣簡短的敘事，都比交錯的將事實和個人意見參雜在一起，更能有效抓住讀者的興趣。

## 整理出相關事件和時間

當公司內部發生嚴重的糾紛時，律師通常會請客戶「依時間順序說明相關事件」，並對引發糾紛的最關鍵事件做詳細說明。這樣的紀錄文件能幫每位當事人釐清事情的前因後果。當你在寫文件時，無論是寫信說明專案的最新進度，或是準備員工的績效考核，都可試著採用類似的方法，帶領讀者依序了解一連串事件。依時間順序梳理相關事件，可協助建立敘事架構。假設在寫右邊範例中那封給莎拉的信之前，你依時間整理出各個事件，時間表可能會如下表所示：

## Chronology of relevant events 相關事件時間表

| | |
|---|---|
| **Last week**<br>**上週** | Sarah asked me to gauge Magnabilify's interest in having us build customized security applications.<br>莎拉要我評估 Magnabilify 對我們建立的客製化安全應用程式是否感興趣。 |
| **Today**<br>**今天** | I spoke with Jim Martinez.<br>與吉姆馬丁尼茲商談此事。 |
| **Next Tuesday**<br>**下週二** | Jim and I will meet at his office to discuss.<br>與吉姆約在他的辦公室討論。 |
| **In two weeks**<br>**兩週後** | If Magnabilify is interested, we'll do an NDA, develop a sample app, and schedule a demo.<br>如果 Magnabilify 有興趣，我們會簽訂保密協議、開發應用程式樣本和安排演示時間。 |

像這樣列出事件後，再動手寫信就變得容易許多，只要依序說明事件，再要求與莎拉在下週二開會前先約時間面談，這封信便大功告成。

### 重點回顧

- 只提及相關的事實。
- 依時間順序列出事件，讓讀者可輕鬆了解事件全貌。
- 在下筆之前，整理相關事件時間表，以組織敘事架構，接著便可依序說明事件。但應避免機械式的寫出不必要的日期。

第 13 章

# 確保文章連貫性

## Be a stickler for continuity

流暢的寫作呈現的是一連串組織得宜的句子和段落，而不僅只是字句的堆疊。這種順暢的承接講究的是完善的規劃和處理轉折的技巧，或是能讓讀者跟上你思路的連結性。

曼努埃爾G．維拉斯奎茲（Manuel G. Velasquez）是位出色的作家。以下是他在撰寫關於商業倫理（Business Ethics）時，各段落的第一句話。一起來看看他是如何做到順暢的銜接（轉折的連接用字以斜體標示）：

**曼努埃爾G．維拉斯奎茲**

《商業倫理》（2011）各段落的第一句話

1. ***How well*** does a free monopoly market succeed in achieving the moral values that characterize perfectly competitive free markets? Not well.

2. The ***most obvious failure*** of monopoly markets lies in the high prices they enable the monopolist to charge and the high profits they enable him to reap, a failure that violates capitalist justice.
3. A monopoly market ***also*** results in a decline in the efficiency with which it allocates and distributes goods.
4. ***First***, the monopoly market allows resources to be used in ways that will produce shortages of those things buyers want and cause them to be sold at higher prices than necessary.
5. ***Second***, monopoly markets do not encourage suppliers to use resources in ways that will minimize the resources consumed to produce a certain amount of a commodity.
6. ***Third***, a monopoly market allows the seller to introduce price differentials that block consumers from putting together the most satisfying bundle of commodities they can purchase given the commodities available and the money they can spend.
7. Monopoly markets ***also*** embody restrictions on the negative rights that perfectly free markets respect.
8. A monopoly market, ***then***, is one that deviates from the ideals of capitalist justice, economic utility, and negative rights.

1. 道德價值觀是完全自由競爭市場的一大特色，自由獨占市場**是否成功**實現這種道德價值觀呢？答案是否定的。
2. 獨占市場**最明顯的失敗**在於壟斷者可收取高額價格，獲取高額利潤，完全違背了資本主義的正義。
3. 獨占市場**同時也**導致分配和經銷商品的效率低落。
4. **首先**，獨占市場的資源使用方式導致買方想買的商品短缺，進而使得商品價格高得超乎尋常。
5. **其次**，獨占市場不鼓勵供應商以最少的資源製造一定數量的商品。
6. **再者**，獨占市場的賣方可透過價格差異化，讓消費者無法根據可購買的商品和可花用預算，買到屬意的商品組合。
7. **此外**，獨占市場也對完全自由市場所尊重的消極權利造成了限制。
8. **由此可知**，獨占市場偏離了資本主義正義、經濟效用和消極權利的理想。

這些以斜體標示的轉折詞（transitional phrases）引導著我們從一個觀點，前往下一個觀點。一般來說，我們甚至不會注意到這些詞。在真正高明的寫作中，幾乎察覺不到轉折詞的存在，但它們其實是被精心安排在讀者需要的地方。這類連接字詞可透過不同方式帶領讀者前進，包括：

## 建立時間順序

| | | | | |
|---|---|---|---|---|
| then<br>然後 | at that point<br>在那時 | afterward<br>之後 | as soon as<br>一…就… | at last<br>最後 |
| before<br>在…之前 | after<br>在…之後 | first<br>首先 | initially<br>起初 | meanwhile<br>同時 |
| later<br>之後 | next<br>接下來 | now<br>現在 | once<br>一旦 | originally<br>原本 |
| since<br>自從 | then<br>接著 | until<br>直到 | until<br>直到 | |

## 建立空間感

| | | | | |
|---|---|---|---|---|
| there<br>那裡 | in that place<br>在那個地方 | at the front<br>在前面 | in back<br>在後面 | farther back<br>更後面 |
| in the rear<br>在後方 | at the center<br>在中心 | to the left (right)<br>在左邊（右邊） | up front<br>在前面 | way back<br>遠遠的在後面 |

## 補充論點

| | | | | |
|---|---|---|---|---|
| and<br>和／而且 | or<br>或 | further<br>進一步 | also<br>也 | in fact<br>事實上 |
| moreover<br>此外 | not only... but also...<br>不僅…而且… | | | |

## 強調論點

| | | | | |
|---|---|---|---|---|
| above all<br>最重要的是 | after all<br>畢竟 | and so<br>因此 | chiefly<br>主要是 | equally important<br>同樣重要的是 |
| more so<br>更是如此 | indeed<br>確實 | more important<br>更重要的是 | | |

## 承認論點

| | | | | |
|---|---|---|---|---|
| although<br>雖然 | and yet<br>然而 | admittedly<br>誠然 | at the same time<br>同時 | certainly<br>當然 |
| even though<br>即使 | doubtless<br>無疑 | granted<br>誠然 | no doubt<br>毫無疑問 | of course<br>當然 |
| still<br>仍然 | though<br>雖然 | to be sure<br>的確 | whereas<br>然而 | yet<br>但是 |
| while<br>而 | | | | |

## 回到之前的論點

| | | | |
|---|---|---|---|
| even so<br>即便如此 | nevertheless<br>然而 | nonetheless<br>儘管如此 | still<br>仍然 |

## 舉例說明

| | | |
|---|---|---|
| for example<br>例如 | for instance<br>舉例來說 | in particular<br>特別是 |

## 提供原因

| | | | | |
|---|---|---|---|---|
| because<br>因為 | hence<br>因此 | thus<br>因而 | for<br>因為 | it follows<br>由此可見 |
| since<br>由於 | so<br>所以 | then<br>那麼 | therefore<br>因此 | |

## 表達對比

| | | | | |
|---|---|---|---|---|
| but<br>但是 | yet<br>然而 | and yet<br>然而 | conversely<br>相反的 | despite<br>儘管 |
| by contrast<br>相較之下 | instead<br>反而 | on the other hand<br>另一方面 | still<br>仍然 | then<br>然後<br>（但有時可表示轉折） |
| while<br>而 | | | | |

## 作出總結

| | | | | |
|---|---|---|---|---|
| so<br>所以 | as a result<br>結果 | finally<br>最後 | in conclusion<br>總結來說 | in short<br>簡而言之 |
| in sum<br>總而言之 | on the whole<br>整體而言 | therefore<br>因此 | thus<br>因此 | to sum up<br>總結 |

## 善用副標題作為轉折

然而，無論你的句子和段落銜接得再順暢，如果在讀者眼前是一大段的文字，趕時間的讀者還是無法集中精神閱讀。所以，要善用小標題將內容分成不同部分（即使只是超過一段的電子郵件也適用），引導讀者逐一讀過，並協助他們快速找出感興趣的部分。比方說，看到「摘要」（summary）這個副標題，讀者就知道可以在此找到重點。此外，簡潔明瞭的副標題可呈現重點，讓讀者即使快速瀏覽，依然能夠掌握訊息要點。

撰寫副標題時盡可能統一句型。舉例來說，假設你帶領一個工作小組，要針對如何透過社群媒體直接建立顧客關係提供建議，你可以用祈使句為內文中的每個副標題下標，例如：

Use LinkedIn to Get Feedback on Current Products

使用LinkedIn取得最新產品的意見回饋

Use Facebook to Test New Concepts

使用Facebook測試新概念

Use X to Facilitate Chats About Live Events

使用X（前稱Twitter）讓討論時事更容易

這樣的排比句能讓你的文章無論在修辭或邏輯上，都顯得更前後一致。

## 重點回顧

- 善用安排得當的轉折詞將讀者帶往下一個論點，並說明與前述論點的關係。
- 運用簡潔且清楚描述內容的副標題來將文章分段，以提高可讀性，並協助讀者快速找出最重要的資訊。
- 利用「摘要」副標題引導讀者查看文章的重點。
- 在副標題採用一致的風格和排比句型，以加強文章在邏輯和修辭上的連貫性。

## • NOTE •

第 14 章

# 學好基礎正確文法

Learn the basics of correct grammar

為什麼要特別講究文法？因為對讀者來說，你的文字運用，所反映的是你的能力。如果你的文章錯誤百出，別人會覺得你愚昧無知，進而對可否信任你的建議感到遲疑，例如要啟動一項需要大量資源的專案，或是採購某項商品或服務。他們可能會認為你連自己在說什麼都不知道。

## 常見的指標性錯誤

使用代名詞時，多想一想。如果你不懂得如何使用 I 和 me，你的同事、合作夥伴和客戶多半也不會認真把你當一回事。可以想見，有些錯誤可能會給你帶來麻煩：

| ✕ 錯誤說法： | ○ 正確說法： |
|---|---|
| She placed an order *with Megan and *I*. | She placed an order with Megan and ***me***.<br>她向我和梅根下訂單。 |

| | |
|---|---|
| （電話中：）*This is ***him***. | This is ***he***.<br>我就是。 |
| Just keep this matter *between you and ***I***. | Just keep this matter between you and ***me***.<br>這件事是你和我之間的祕密。 |
| ****Whom*** may I say is calling? | ***Who*** may I say is calling?<br>請問哪裡找？ |

此處的規則非常簡單，

| 說明： | 例句： |
|---|---|
| **I、we、he和she是子句的主詞** | Leslie and I were delighted to work with you.<br>萊斯利和我很高興與你共事。 |
| **me、us、him和her則是動詞或介系詞的受詞** | Please call either Leslie or me.<br>請來電找萊斯利或我。<br>You might want to consult with Leslie and me.<br>你可以向萊斯利和我諮詢。 |

只要試著把複合詞組中的Leslie and拿掉，正確的用法馬上就呼之欲出。

除了代名詞的問題外，以下是幾個須留意的主要文法錯誤類型。至於其他更多可能損及你公信力的用字問題，請參見附錄D和F。

## 主詞動詞不一致

動詞必須與主詞的人稱和單複數一致<I am aware of that>（我知道那件事）、<You are aware of that>（你知道那件事）、<Pat is aware of that>（派特知道那件事）、<We are all aware of that>（我們都知道那件事），但句子結構可能會使問題變得複雜。

There is的句型常會讓人搞錯，因為There看起來是主詞，其實不然。這個字是文法學家所謂的“expletive”，不是指髒話的expletive（例如“expletive deleted”表示已刪去髒話），而是在倒裝句中用來當作主詞的填充詞。

在這類句子中，there is就是「有」的意思，例如：There is a vacancy on the hiring committee.（招聘委員會有一個空缺。）若改為非倒裝句則是：A vacancy (exists) on the hiring committee. 因為there在有些人看來像是單數主詞，因此他們常會使用單數動詞。但there是把字序顛倒，真正的主詞其實在動詞之後<There are several reasons for approving the plan>（批准這項計畫有幾個理由）。因此，當主詞是複數時，當然必須用複數動詞。

| ✕ 錯誤示範： | | ○ 正確示範： |
|---|---|---|
| There ***is*** always risk and liability ***considerations*** to take into account. | ▶ | There ***are*** always risk and liability ***considerations*** to take into account.<br>總是有風險和責任因素必須納入考量。 |

| | |
|---|---|
| There ***is*** many ***options*** to avoid a takeover. | There ***are*** many ***options*** to avoid a takeover.<br>有許多選項可避免收購。 |

另一個棘手的主詞與動詞不一致問題，發生在主詞後面接有介系詞片語時。由於「受假象吸引」，寫作者常會被誤導而選錯動詞（以單數動詞搭配複數主詞，或複數動詞搭配單數主詞）。介系詞片語的受詞從來都不是句子的主詞，它們可能較靠近動詞，但動詞的單複數應取決於主詞：

| ✕ 錯誤示範： | ○ 正確示範： |
|---|---|
| The ***details*** of the customized work is ***delaying*** the project. | The ***details*** of the customized work ***are delaying*** the project.<br>客製化工作的細節拖延了專案的進度。 |
| The ***source*** of our replacement parts and maintenance ***have not been selected*** yet. | The ***source*** for our replacement parts and maintenance supplies ***has not been selected*** yet.<br>尚未選擇替換零件和維修用品的來源。 |

在第一個例句中，work是介系詞of的受詞，所以動詞應該與複數主詞details一致。在第二個例句，source決定了動詞為單數的has not been selected。

用or、either...or或neither...nor連接多個主詞時，也可能出現不一致的情況。如果所有主詞皆為單數，則動詞亦為單數。但若其中一或多個主詞為複數，**動詞的單複數則必須與or或nor後的名詞單複數一致：**

| ✕ 錯誤示範： | | ○ 正確示範： |
| --- | --- | --- |
| Special services ***or*** a new product ***target*** a niche market. | ▶ | Special services ***or*** a new product ***targets*** a niche market.<br>特殊服務或新產品鎖定的是小眾市場。 |
| ***Neither*** the education fund ***nor*** the training costs ***is*** without budget constraints. | ▶ | ***Neither*** the education fund ***nor*** the training costs ***are*** without budget constraints.<br>教育基金和培訓成本並非沒有預算限制。 |

在第一個例句中，or之後的單數主詞a new product決定了應使用單數動詞。在第二個例句，也是由nor之後的複數主詞決定應該用複數動詞。請注意，使用「單數主詞or複數主詞+複數動詞」的形式，是較自然常見的用法。

## 名詞與代名詞不一致

嚴格來說，代名詞必須與主詞的性別和單複數一致。

| ✕ 錯誤示範： | ○ 正確示範： |
|---|---|
| A ***shareholder*** may cast ***their*** vote for only one member of the board. | A ***shareholder*** may cast ***his or her*** vote for only one member of the board.<br>一名股東只能投票給一名董事會成員。 |

**雖然口語上會將their用作無性別的單數代名詞，但在正式寫作中，這還不是廣為人接受的用法。**而除非明確知道主詞的性別，否則也應避免使用男性或女性代名詞。如果你想用性別代名詞來表明政治立場（例如一律選擇泛指女性的代名詞），你大可這麼做；但你要知道，這麼做可能會讓部分讀者分心，或有可能使你的公信力大打折扣。**最安全的做法是花點巧思，以不提及性別的中性寫法帶過。**

| ✕ 錯誤示範： | ○ 正確示範： |
|---|---|
| ***Either*** the receptionist or the sales assistant will have to change ***their*** lunch hour so that at least one will be in the office at all times.<br>接待人員或銷售助理必須有其中一位調整午餐時間，以確保無論何時都至少有一人在辦公室。 | ***Either*** the receptionist or the sales assistant will have to start taking lunch earlier or later so that at least one will be in the office at all times.<br>接待人員或銷售助理必須有其中一位提早或延後用餐，以確保無論何時都至少有一人在辦公室。 |

| × 錯誤示範： | | ○ 正確示範： |
|---|---|---|
| ***Three candidates*** responded to the advertisement for the financial-officer position. ***Each*** submitted ***their*** résumé. | ▶ | ***Three candidates*** responded to the advertisement for the financial-officer position. ***Each*** submitted ***a*** résumé.<br>有三位應徵者回覆財務主管職位的徵人廣告，每位都附上了履歷。 |

再說回文法上，當句子主詞是either、neither、each或every這類單數代名詞時，其後所接的其他名詞並不影響動詞的單複數：

| × 錯誤示範： | | ○ 正確示範： |
|---|---|---|
| ***Have either*** of our clients arrived yet? | ▶ | ***Has either*** of our clients arrived yet?<br>有任何一位客戶抵達了嗎？ |
| ***Neither*** of the new products ***have*** sold spectacularly this year. | ▶ | ***Neither*** of the new products ***has*** sold spectacularly this year.<br>今年沒有任何一款新品銷售出色。 |
| ***Each*** of us ***are*** responsible for the tasks assigned. | ▶ | ***Each*** of us ***is*** responsible for the tasks assigned.<br>我們每個人各自負責獲指派的任務。 |

## 雙重否定

若連用兩個否定字來強調否定的意涵，而非相互抵銷，即形成所謂「雙重否定」。這種情形在方言中很容易看出（例如：we didn't have no choice或it didn't hardly matter），但在正式寫作中的問題則可能較不易察覺。多留意當not加上其他含有否定意涵的字。

| ✕ 錯誤示範： | ○ 正確示範： |
| --- | --- |
| We ***couldn't scarcely*** manage to keep up with the demand.<br>我們幾乎無法趕不上需求。 | We ***could scarcely*** manage to keep up with the demand.<br>我們幾乎趕不上需求。（scarecely表示「幾乎不」） |

另一個不易察覺的雙重否定組合是not...but。

| ✕ 錯誤示範： | ○ 正確示範： |
| --- | --- |
| The clerk ***couldn't*** help ***but*** call the manager for advice. | The clerk ***couldn't*** help calling the manager for advice.<br>店員不得不打電話向經理尋求建議。 |

But可表示否定，也可用於表示對比，所以用not...but可能會使語意模稜兩可。上例中的第一個句子可能意指店員還有其他選擇，第二句則明白指出店員別無選擇。

## 非標準詞彙

在商業寫作中，除非是特地為少數非使用標準英語的對象而寫，否則請一律使用標準英語。廣義來說，標準英語是指在文法、字彙、拼字和標點符號等方面，留意使用一般可接受的常規用法。

不是要你非得嚴格遵守正式寫法，在適當的情況下，也可使用較不正式的英語，但你的文章和言詞一定要專業得體。

方言向來是非標準用法，應避免在商業寫作中使用：

| ✕ 錯誤示範： | | ○ 正確示範： |
| --- | --- | --- |
| ***Where's*** the meeting ***at***? | ▶ | ***Where's*** the meeting?<br>開會地點在哪裡？ |
| ***Me and Kim*** will handle the Brewster account. | ▶ | ***Kim and I*** will handle the Brewster account.<br>金和我會處理布魯斯特的帳號。 |

寫作者若仰賴口語發音來拼寫單字，也可能會冒出非標準用字：

| ✕ 錯誤示範： | | ○ 正確示範： |
| --- | --- | --- |
| They ***shouldn't of*** submitted those incomplete reports. | ▶ | They ***shouldn't have*** submitted those incomplete reports.<br>他們不應該提交那些不完整的報告。 |

不規則動詞是另一個容易孕育出非標準用語的溫床。

| ✕ 錯誤示範： | | ○ 正確示範： |
| --- | --- | --- |
| We ***drug*** our heels getting into the mid-Atlantic market. | ▶ | We ***dragged*** our heels getting into the mid-Atlantic market.<br>我們慢吞吞的打進中大西洋幾州的市場。 |
| Our late entry almost ***sunk*** our chances against established competitors. | ▶ | Our late entry almost ***sank*** our chances against established competitors.<br>我們太晚打入市場幾乎讓我們失去與既有競爭對手競爭的機會。 |

## 如何自我改正錯誤

以下三個好方法可有助於修改文章：（1）閱讀優秀的非小說讀物；（2）請學問好的同事幫忙校對，並說明修改的理由；以及（3）閱讀文法書和用法指南，有問題時隨時查閱。

上述最後一個方法可協助你辨別真正的規則，和令人深受其擾的假規則。舉例來說，你在學校時是否曾學過句子絕不能以連接詞開頭？我也是。但看看那些一流的文章，多的是以and和but開頭的句子，這樣的句子無所不在。以這類連接詞開頭的句子，可保持讀者的思路順暢。無論現在或過去，這麼做都沒有違反任何規則。

就文法來說，以additionally和however作為句子開頭沒有什麼不對。但就風格上來說，較不建議這種寫法，因為與單音節的連接詞相比，多音節的字無法達到一樣俐落緊密的承接效果。

或許你會擔心讀者會認為句子以連接詞開頭是錯的？其實讀者根本不會注意，就像你從來也不曾注意一樣。好的寫作風格會讓讀者專注在你簡潔明瞭的訊息上，相較之下，拙劣的寫作風格，才會吸引讀者注意到風格本身。

如需可方便參考的文法指南，請參閱附錄B〈不可不知的十二條文法規則〉，並請務必花點時間仔細詳讀附錄F〈正確用字入門〉。當你對語言投以熱愛，它也會給你相同的回報。

## 重點回顧

- 考慮動詞的單複數時，應多留意複合型的主詞、倒裝句型，以及主詞後的介系詞片語。
- 不要將介系詞的受詞誤認為句子的主詞。
- 在正式寫作中，避免將they/them/their作為無性別的單數代名詞。
- 避免使用雙重否定。
- 遵循標準英語的習慣用法。
- 多讀優質的非小說讀物、請同事過目你寫的內容，並在遇到問題時參考文法書和用法指南，以加強對標準英語的掌握。

## • NOTE •

第 15 章

# 請求同事提供意見

Get feedback on your drafts from colleagues

假設你草擬了一份預算申請文件，你可以請同組成員看過一遍，確認內容是否夠清楚簡潔且夠有說服力，能充分說明為何應核撥經費，讓你們再多請兩名員工。如果可以，不妨也向其他部門立場客觀的同仁尋求有建設性的回饋，最好是找擅長透過遊說取得資源的人。

好好記下同事的說法，他們的回應可能和你目標讀者的看法不謀而合。

## 有禮的接受建議

優秀的寫作者對好的修改建議歡迎之至，甚至是求之不得；差勁的寫作者則對此充滿憎恨，只會將他人的建議視為人身攻擊。優秀的寫作者靈感源源不絕，因此不會把自己的想法看得太重；差勁的寫作者因為靈感匱乏，所以把每個想法都看得彌足珍貴。因此建議在稿子初具雛形時就與他人分享，旁人的意見可有助於更快釐清脈絡，好過你獨自苦思琢磨。

**盡量避免讓同事當面說明修改的原因**，因為當面指正可能會讓人產生自我防禦，而無法聽進好的建議。**你可以請他們標註在文件上**，並別忘感謝他們的幫忙。

如果定期要求下屬修改你的文章，使其更簡潔有力，你會獲得兩個好處：你的文章會更加精練，下屬也會因為練習而成為更好的編輯者和寫作者。但你必須為他們指明方向：告訴他們不只要找出明顯的錯誤，還要能指出太冗長、不清楚，或在表達上顯得突兀的地方。最理想的狀況是，他們提出的建議有百分之八十你都可以接受。

## 打造樂於修改校訂的文化

在我的公司，負責編輯或校對的人每頁至少必須提出兩個修改建議。沒有人能在交回稿件時說一句「看起來沒問題！」，就算只是一封簡短的信也不例外。問問自己「有什麼作者該說而沒說到的地方？語氣可以再怎麼改進？有沒有更貼切、更簡短的措詞能說明這個想法？」，藉由提出問題，一定能找出可加強的地方。

如果每個看過的人每頁都至少要提出兩個修改建議，相信我，錯字一定無所遁形。錯字一般最容易發現，所以在嘗試提出較困難的風格改善建議之前，讀者通常會先找出錯字。到最後，任何不流暢的問題都會消失。你和你的團隊會因為表現優異，而顯得更出色。你的論點會更明確有力，簡報也會更具有說服力。

這麼做算是矯枉過正嗎？想一想，你發出的所有通訊內容，都代表你的團隊或公司，以及你們的專業形象。如果這是會大量散佈的印刷手冊或商務信函，眾人的反饋意見更是多多益善，就算叫再多雙銳利的鷹眼來幫忙檢查都不為過。

犯下低級錯誤可能會帶來災難性的後果。曾有一所主要大學在印了數千本畢業典禮的宣傳冊後，才發現封面上大大的印著「School of Pubic Affairs」的錯字。這個尷尬錯字的相片幾乎立刻出現在網路上，這所大學自然也成為許多人的笑柄。

所以說到寫作，我們希望打造理性互助的文化。需要其他人的編輯建議沒什麼好丟臉，我們都應該自在的尋求或給予建議，不帶有任何令人不快、自認高人一等的意味。組織中的每個人，無論職位高低，都能從好的修改建議中獲益。

## 重點回顧

- 固定請同事和下屬幫忙看你的稿子並提出修改建議。
- 請他們將修改建議用寫的標註在文件上，避免當面提出意見，以免產生防禦心理。一定要記得謝謝他們的協助。
- 打造一個可自在尋求和提供修改建議的環境，沒有小心眼的互相競爭意味。

• NOTE •

- Section -

# 3

# 避免怪異的寫作習慣讓目標讀者失去興趣

Avoiding the Quirks That Turn Readers Off

第 16 章

# 不要讓目標讀者感到昏昏欲睡

## Don't anesthetize your readers

不要讓閱讀對象看你寫的東西看到想睡，這點不必多說，想必大家都知道。那些在晚餐聚會上講話拐彎抹角，或是發表無聊演說的人，應該也都懂這個道理，但想想你曾經被迫聽過多少無聊的演講。其實無論是對話或寫作，情況大可不必如此。

仔細回想你曾遇過最會聊天的對象，或最厲害的講者。無論多冷僻的主題，他們都有辦法講得生動有趣。他們不用老掉牙的表達方式，愛用簡單有力的字。想想邱吉爾那句關於「熱血、辛勞、眼淚和汗水」（blood, toil, tears, and sweat）的名言。也別忘了據說華盛頓被問到那棵被砍倒的櫻桃樹時，他是怎麼說的：他不是說「用一把邊緣鋒利的小型工具完成的」"It was accomplished by utilizing a small sharp-edged implement."，而是「用我那把小斧頭砍的」"I used my little hatchet."。

厲害的寫作者使用的也是相同技巧。為什麼有些書讓人欲罷不能，有些書卻被擱置在一旁？關鍵在於風格：作者解釋事情和說故事的風格。

以下提供幾個在撰寫商業文件時，可抓住對方注意力的祕訣。

## 有技巧的使用人稱代名詞

不要過度使用I這個字（盡量避免以I作為段落開頭，或連著幾句話都以I開始），但可多用we、our、you和your。這些都是表達親近友好的字，可顯得更具有人情味，吸引對方專注投入於文章中。《How to Be Brief》一書的作者魯道夫弗雷奇是提倡簡明英語的代表人物，也是最早解釋使用you的必要性的其中一人：

持續的與你的閱讀對象對話。任何時候，都盡可能使用第二人稱代名詞，將每句話都以you來改寫。例如，

| 原本寫法： | 建議寫法： |
|---|---|
| ***This*** applies to citizens over 65.<br>這點適用於65歲以上的公民。 | If ***you're*** over 65, this applies to ***you***.<br>如果你年滿65歲，這點即適用於你。 |
| ***It*** must be remembered that...<br>請務必記得… | ***You*** must remember...<br>你務必記得… |
| ***Many people*** don't realize...<br>很多人不能理解… | Perhaps ***you*** don't realize...<br>或許你不能理解… |

寫作時，一律直接以你要傳達訊息的那個人，you，為對象。

同樣的，當我們用we和our來指稱自己的公司，可讓公司（和其他的法律實體）聽起來像是有共同的性格（公司確實應該也通常有自

己的性格）。比起用呆板疏遠的第三人稱代名詞來自稱，這種親切沒有距離的說法通常更受人青睞。試比較以下兩個例子：

**✕ 錯誤示範：**

Whether or not ***a stockholder*** plans to attend a meeting, ***he or she*** should take the time to vote by completing and mailing the enclosed proxy card to ***the Company***. If ***a stockholder*** signs, dates, and mails a proxy card without indicating how ***he or she*** wants to vote, ***that stockholder***'s proxy will be counted as a vote in favor of the merger. If ***a stockholder*** fails to return a proxy card, the effect in most cases will be a vote against the merger.

無論股東是否打算出席會議，都請撥冗填寫隨附的委託書並寄回以參與投票。如果股東簽署、標註日期並寄回的委託書未指出欲投票的選項，該股東的委託書將會視為贊成併購。若股東未寄回委託書，在多數情況下則會視為反對併購。

**○ 正確示範：**

Whether or not ***you*** plan to attend a meeting, please take the time to vote by completing and mailing the enclosed proxy card to ***us***. If ***you*** sign, date, and mail ***your*** proxy card without indicating how ***you*** want to vote, ***your*** proxy will count as a vote in favor of the merger. If ***you*** don't return ***your*** card, in most cases ***you'll*** be counted as voting against the merger.

無論你是否打算出席會議，都請撥冗填寫隨附的委託書並寄回以參與投票。如果簽署、標註日期並寄回的委託書未指出欲投票的選項，委託書將一律視為贊成併購。若未寄回委託書，在多數情況下則會視為反對併購。

## 使用縮讀字（contractions）

許多寫作者對使用縮讀字有種莫名的害怕，可能是因為以前學校教我們要避免使用。但其實用縮讀字並未違反任何真正的規則，反而可化解文章的窒悶感，這點正是許多人寫作寫不好的主要原因。

但這只是要你放輕鬆寫，而不是要你變得輕佻，或使用大量俚語。當你說話時會選擇縮讀，寫作時就可用縮讀字；如果不會，就不用縮讀字。

| ✕ 錯誤示範： | ○ 正確示範： |
| --- | --- |
| For those customers who do not participate in West Bank's online banking program, and do not wish to consider doing so, West Bank will continue sending them statements by U.S. Mail.<br>對於尚未加入且無意加入西部銀行網路銀行方案的顧客，西部銀行會繼續透過美國郵政寄送對帳單。 | If you prefer not to use our online banking program, we'll continue mailing your statements to you.<br>若你不想使用網路銀行方案，我們會繼續以郵寄方式提供對帳單。 |
| We would like to remind you that it is not necessary to be present to win. We will inform all winners by telephone subsequent to the drawing.<br>在此提醒你，中獎與否和是否出席無關，我們會在抽獎後致電通知所有得獎者。 | Remember: You needn't be present to win the drawing. We'll call you if you win.<br>注意：中獎與否和是否出席無關，我們會致電通知得獎者。 |

## 堅守用字簡單的原則

我知道我已經說過很多次，但這點即使說再多遍都不為過。對方若是無法理解你的內容，就會放棄嘗試閱讀。

## 避免使用被動語態

不要說"The closing documents were prepared by Sue."(交屋文件是由蘇所準備。),可改成"Sue prepared the closing documents."(蘇準備了交屋文件。);不要說"The message was sent by George."(訊息是喬治所寄出。),可以說"George sent the message."(喬治寄出了訊息。)或"The message came from George."(訊息來自喬治。)。

不過這項準則並非絕對,有時就是得用被動語態才是最自然的說法,比如說:Sometimes it can't be avoided.(有時這是無法避免的。)但若能養成盡量使用主動語態的習慣,可讓你在很大程度上避免寫出複雜難懂、不流暢的句子。

要怎麼辨別被動語態呢?只要記得被動語態一定是be動詞(通常是is、are、was、were)或get,加上過去式動詞。be動詞共有八個,過去分詞則有無數個。

### 被動語態範例

- is + delivered 被遞送
- are + finished 被完成
- was + awarded 被獎勵
- were + praised 被誇讚
- been + adjusted 被調整
- being + flown 被空運
- be + served 被服務
- am + relieved 被緩解
- got + promoted 被升職

只要盡量減少使用被動語態，你的寫作就能有所提升。（You will improve your writing if you minimize passive voice.）（可別把這句話說成：Your writing will be improved if passive voice is minimized by you.）

## 變化句子長度和結構

羅馬哲學家西塞羅曾說過，統一單調會使人感到枯燥乏味。這句話不只適用於飲食和其他所有事物，套用到句型上也一樣適用。一成不變令人厭煩。正因如此，寫作時得要有長句，也要有短句；要有主要子句（main clauses），也要有附屬子句（subordinate clauses）。豐富多變才是王道。

| ✕ 錯誤示範： | ○ 正確示範： |
| --- | --- |
| Over a significant period of time, we have gained experience helping our clients improve operational performance and maximize both the efficiency of their human resources and the economical utilization of their capital. Ours is an integrated approach that both diagnoses and streamlines operating practices and procedures using lean maintenance and optimization tools, while at the same time implementing change-management techniques involving mind-sets and behaviors of those involved in managerial positions within a given organization. | For many years, we have helped clients better use their resources and improve performance. How? By streamlining operations and changing managers' mind-sets and behaviors.<br><br>多年來，我們幫助許多客戶更妥善的運用資源並提升成效。怎麼做到呢？靠著精簡作業和改變管理人員的思維和行為。 |

| ✕ 錯誤示範： | ○ 正確示範： |
| --- | --- |
| 這麼長的時間以來，對於協助客戶提升營運成效，改善效率和人力資源，以及經濟實惠的運用經費，我們已累積相當多的經驗。我們的做法是透過精益維修和最佳化工具，將診斷及精簡作業程序和流程整合，同時針對特定組織管理階層的思維和行為，施行管理改造技巧。 | |

| ✕ 錯誤示範： | ○ 正確示範： |
| --- | --- |
| In order to provide you, the user of our products, the option of obtaining free replacements for defective products from the nearest office, we offer a simplified processing without acknowledgment of the statutory duty ("goodwill") regardless of whether the product has been purchased there or has reached the user by another route.<br><br>為了讓我們的產品用戶可選擇在最近的營業處免費更換有問題的產品，無論產品是否在該營業處購買，或是透過其他途徑送到使用者手上，我們都可在未承認法定義務的前提下（即善意處理），提供更簡便的流程。 | What should you do if you need a free replacement for a defective product? Go to the nearest office. Any of our offices can help even if you did not purchase the item there.<br><br>如果要免費更換有問題的產品，該怎麼做？請前往最近的營業處，即使不是在該處購買，任何一間營業處都會協助處理。 |

## 避免使用大量首字母縮寫（acronym）

使用首字母縮寫會讓你的閱讀對象看得很累，尤其如果對方對那些縮寫並不熟悉，因此對於縮寫應審慎使用。比起拼寫出cost of goods sold（銷貨成本），只寫COGS對你可能更省事，但若是將ABC（activity-based costing，作業基礎成本制）、EBITDA（earnings before interest, tax, depreciation, and amortization，稅息折舊及攤銷前利潤）和VBM（value-based management，價值管理）等縮寫也一股腦拋出，從事會計工作的人或許能夠理解，卻會讓你失去其他人的注意力。這一點也不奇怪，因為對方不會為了想看懂你在說什麼，而去學習那些艱澀的詞彙。

在閱讀時，你一定有過這樣的經驗：你看到一個首字母縮寫（運氣特別差的話，可能還是個很長的縮寫），而就目前文章或文件所讀到的部分，看不出與它關聯的字詞。於是，你往前翻找看過的內容，希望能找到此縮寫第一次出現的地方，或是與之相符的文字。等到你終於找到（或放棄尋找）時，你已經完全忘了作者要說什麼。千萬不要讓你的閱讀對象也經歷一樣的情況。

能逐字寫出，就不要用縮寫。使用縮寫方便了你，卻苦了對方。別讓你的捷徑成為對方的障礙。

### 重點回顧

- 不要太常用I，倒是可以多用we、our、you和your，這樣可讓文章讀來更親切、更吸引對方。
- 克服對使用縮讀字的恐懼，可讓你的文章擺脫窒悶感。
- 除非在特定情況下，被動語態聽起來更自然，否則應盡量使用主動語態，讓文章更清楚直白。
- 為句子的長度和結構多加點變化。
- 盡可能避免使用首字母縮寫，讓閱讀對象可輕鬆的閱讀。

第 17 章

# 注意寫作的語氣

Watch your tone

掌握對的寫作語氣並不容易，但卻是一篇商業文件成功與否的關鍵。專業討喜的語氣，會讓人樂於與你合作及給予回覆。因此建議採用較輕鬆自在的語氣，就像是直接與文件的目標讀者對話。

## 避免過度正式

如果有同事說出或寫出“How may I be of assistance?”（我能為您做些什麼？）這樣的句子，而不是“How may I help you?”（我能為您效勞嗎？），或寫出 “subsequent to our conversation”（在我們談話之後），而不是“after we spoke”（在我們交談之後），你會作何感想？當他們在過分誇張的用字和日常口語用字間選擇了前者，你會不會覺得他們太過浮誇自大？

太正式的語氣會破壞風格。試試透過以下做法，保持親切真誠的寫作風格：

- 以平時說話的語氣來撰寫內容，但仍應避免太隨興的口頭禪（例如like和you know）。

- 多用thank you、we're happy to和we appreciate，以保持有禮的態度。
- 若要提到某人，可直接寫出其姓名（例如David Green，而不是above-mentioned patient「前文所提到的病人」）。
- 使用人稱代名詞（以you、he、she來指稱，而不是the reader, the decedent, the applicant「那位讀者、死者、應徵者」；可以說we understand，而不是it is understood；可說we recommend，不要說it is recommended by the undersigned「這是由屬名人推薦的」）。

## 保持合作友好的態度

當你用合作友善的語氣與人溝通，相信你在傳達大多數訊息時，即使是較難讓人接受的訊息，應該也都能順利傳達。想像一下，假設在一起備受爭議的訴訟中，你寫的任何內容都會呈交在陪審團面前，你一定希望自己在陪審團眼中是個言行得體的人。當然，有時你也必須採取較強硬積極的態度，比如在訴訟進行到最後階段時，但切記這只能作為最後手段，且最好尋求法律顧問的建議。

做你自己，但也得保持最小心謹慎的態度。曾有人因為寫信件、備忘錄或電子郵件時考慮不周，而使公司陷入極大的麻煩，連帶自己的工作也不保。所以，在任何情況下，都要審慎作出最好的判斷。

即使你的態度友善且還算輕鬆，但隨著與目標讀者的關係不同，語氣還是會略有不同。想確保用字恰當，只要問問自己「如果某某某就在旁邊，我會怎麼跟他說這件事？」與最親近的同事說話時，你的口氣不會太疏遠；對於沒那麼熟的人，你也不會用太親密的語氣。

不要想讓你的目標讀者承認他們錯了。用labor under a delusion（抱著錯覺不放）、claim to understand（聲稱理解）、fail to understand

（無法理解）、complain（抱怨）、erroneously assert（錯誤的聲稱）或distort（扭曲事實）來指責對方，是非常不智的行為。像這一類的用詞，只會引起對方的不滿。相反的，應秉持誠信公正的態度來對待讀者，讓他們知道你願意讓步。

## 不要語帶嘲諷

諷刺的語氣給人一種輕蔑且高高在上的感覺。用這種語氣不會使人屈服，倒是一定會惹惱對方，與對方更加疏離。試比較以下例子：

**✕ 錯誤示範：**

Given that Monday was a bank holiday, as declared by federal statute no less, your e-mail of the 17th of the present month did not come to my attention until yesterday. It is with no small degree of regret that we note that you deemed it necessary to send a follow-up e-mail to us regarding this matter, since we are desirous of establishing a relationship of mutual trust and respect.

鑒於星期一是聯邦法規明訂的國定假日，我直到昨天才看到你在本月十七日寄出的電子郵件。看到你認為即使遇到假日也必須寄送後續電子郵件，我們對此深感抱歉，因為我們很希望能與你建立互信互重的關係。

**○ 正確示範：**

Because Monday was a bank holiday, I didn't receive your e-mail message of the 17th until yesterday. Naturally I was chagrined that you had to write a second time. But of course I want you to call on me whenever I might help.

由於星期一是國定假日，我到昨天才收到你在十七日寄的電子郵件。對於你還得為此再寫一封郵件，當然，我感到很抱歉。但當然，若是有我能幫忙的地方，歡迎隨時與我聯絡。

注意到了嗎？左邊的這則範例，是集過度正式和諷刺語氣於一體的死亡組合，還隱含令人惱怒的潛台詞：「你是白痴嗎，在假日寫信來，當然不可能那麼快收到回覆」。至於文末所說「建立互信互重的關係」，想來也是機會渺茫。

## 重點回顧

- 撰寫訊息時，想像自己是當面與目標讀者對話，即可在輕鬆與專業的語氣間取得平衡。
- 對提到的人以其姓名稱呼，並和平常一般自然的使用人稱代名詞，且應避免以太花俏的詞彙取代日常用字。
- 撰寫訊息時，即使是不太正面愉快的內容，也要拿出最好的判斷力和友善的語氣。這可讓你獲得善意的回應，並讓自己和公司都遠離麻煩。
- 根據與目標讀者的關係採用適當的語氣。
- 撰寫專業訊息時，不要語帶諷刺。這樣不會讓你得到想要的結果，反而會適得其反。

- Section -

# 4

# 常見的商業寫作形式

Common Forms of Business Writing

第 18 章

# 電子郵件
E-mails

當你寄送電子郵件時，你通常會收到有用又友善的及時回覆、差強人意的回覆，還是根本毫無回音？如果你為了吸引收件人注意到你的信件所苦，那是因為有太多寄件者在跟你競爭，有時一天甚至多達數百人。

以下說明該如何撰寫電子郵件，才能讓對方真的看進內容、給予回覆並確實採取行動：

- **開門見山直述重點，當然，別忘了保持有禮的態度。**提出要求時別拐彎抹角。雖然幾句簡單的恭維可能很有幫助（例如：「很棒的訪談內容，謝謝分享。對了，可以請你幫個忙嗎？」），但也不要一開頭就過分討好對方。清楚說明期限和收件者需要知道的其他細節，以確保他們可準時做好交辦的工作。
- **審慎選擇副本抄送對象。**確保你加入的收件人都能馬上理解自己收到信的原因，並應避免使用「回覆所有人」。你的「副本」名單中可能已包含太多不相關的收件人，若一直重複這樣的錯誤，會繼續惹惱那些不應該收到信的對象。

- **力求內容精簡扼要。**太長的信件會讓人看得又煩又累。需要捲動或滑動的次數越多，收信者對信件內容的接受度就越低。他們可能只會匆匆看過，因而錯失重要資訊。很多人甚至一看到長信便立即關閉，改從較短的看起。因此，內容盡量不要超過螢幕單一畫面可容納的長度。著重於內容，並精簡用字。
- **信件主旨應短而清楚。**主旨若太過籠統或完全空白，會讓你的信件淹沒於收件人爆量的收件匣中。（不要只寫「計畫」，清楚寫出「11月15日領導人才培訓計畫」。）如果想要求某人做某件事，也應直接在信件主旨註明。讓人一眼就看清楚你的訴求，可達成的機率也會相形提高。
- **依循大小寫和標點符號的標準用法。**對於電子郵件來說，那些好的寫作習慣似乎是在浪費時間，尤其當你是透過行動裝置打出內容。但重點正是在於把事情做對，就算只是一些小事。即使周遭的人在寫信時都不使用大寫字母或標點符號，你也可以擇善固執，自成一格。不按照書面文字常規匆促寫成的郵件，會給人草率大意的印象。太過依賴縮寫，也會使人看了一頭霧水。與其之後再花時間解釋清楚意思，一開始就寫清楚、說明白，會更省時省力得多。
- **使用簽名檔顯示職稱和聯絡資訊。**簽名檔看起來專業最重要（不要太長或太花俏），還要便於讓其他人可選擇如何與你聯絡。

這些訣竅說來都是一般常識，但真正做到的人並不多。為了說明如何實際應用，我們來比較幾則電子郵件範例。

假設你要幫一位初出茅廬的年輕記者朋友爭取實習的機會。你正好認識一家都會報社的編輯，於是你寫了封信給他。試想想以下兩個版本：

**✕ 錯誤示範：**

Subject: Hello there!

Hal—

It's been ages, I know, but I've been meaning to tell you just how effective I think you've been as the editor of the Daily Metropolitan these past seven years. Although I canceled my subscription a few years back (LOL)—the papers kept cluttering the driveway—I buy a copy at the coffee shop almost every day, and I always tell people there just how good the paper is. Who knows, I may have won you some subscribers with all my gushing praise! Believe me, I'm always touting the good old DM.

Anyhoo, I have a mentee I'd like you to meet. You'll soon be thanking me for introducing you to her. She would like an internship, and I know she'll be the best intern you've ever had. Her name is Glenda Jones, and she is A-1 in every way. May I tell her you will contact her? (With good news, I hope!) It can be unpaid. I know your paper has fallen on tough times—but she wants to get into the business anyway! Silly girl. Ah, well, what can you do when journalism seems like it's just in the blood?

Expectantly yours,<br>
Myra

P.S. You'll thank me for this!

主旨：哈囉，你好！

海爾：

我知道，真是好久不見了，但我一直想告訴你，你這七年在《都會日報》擔任編輯的表現真是傑出。雖然我幾年前已經退訂（大笑），因為報紙把車道堆得一團亂，但我幾乎每天都會在咖啡廳買一份來看，而且逢人就推薦這份報紙。誰知道呢，說不定我誇張的讚美曾幫你招攬到一些訂戶！相信我，我向來很推崇這種經典的推銷方式。

不管怎樣，我有指導一位學生，希望你能見見她，很快你就會感謝我把她介紹給你。她想要一個實習的機會，我相信她會是你看過最棒的實習生。她的名字叫葛蘭達瓊斯，各方面的表現都是一流。我可以告訴她你會和她聯絡嗎？（希望會是好消息！）不支薪也可以。我知道你們報社的經濟也很困難，但她還是想走這一行！真傻。唉，如果骨子裡就是對新聞業有興趣，還能怎麼辦呢？

期待你的回覆。
米拉

P.S. 你一定會感謝我的！

## ○ 正確示範：

Subject: Request for an Interview

Hal—

May I ask a favor of you? Glenda Jones, a really sharp mentee in the township's Young Leaders program, wants to pursue a career in journalism, and she's eager to learn how commercial news organizations work. Would you spend 15 minutes chatting with her at your office sometime this month, before school lets out? I know it would be a meaningful introduction for her. You'll find that she is a poised, mature, smart, and incredibly self-possessed young woman.

She tells me that she's looking for an unpaid internship. After a brief interview, perhaps you'd consider giving her a one-week tryout as your assistant. I know you've been a mentor to many aspiring journalists over the years, but here you have a real standout: editor of her college newspaper, Phi Beta Kappa member, state debate champion.

No pressure here. If it's a bad summer for you to take on an intern, I'll completely understand. But please meet with her if you can. I've asked her to write to you independently, enclosing her résumé, to give you a sense of her writing skills.

Thanks very much. Hope you and your family are doing well.

Myra

主旨：面試請求

海爾：

可以請你幫我個忙嗎？鎮上「青年領袖」課程中有一位非常優秀的學生叫葛蘭達瓊斯，她有志從事新聞業，非常渴望能學習商業新聞組織的運作方式。你這個月能空出十五分鐘的時間，在學校放假前，在你辦公室和她聊聊嗎？我相信，這對她來說會是很有意義的介紹。你會發現這個小女生已經做好準備，而且成熟、聰明，又非常有自信。

她跟我說她在找不支薪的實習機會。和她簡短面談之後，或許你可考慮給她一週的時間，試試讓她當你的助理。我知道你這幾年帶過很多有抱負的記者，但她真的非常傑出，她的經歷包括：大學校刊編輯、斐陶斐榮譽學會成員、州際辯論比賽冠軍。

不要有壓力，如果今年夏天不適合帶實習生，我也完全能了解。但是如果可以，請至少和她見一面。我已叫她自己寫信給你，並附上履歷，讓你可看看她的寫作功力。

非常感謝。希望你和你的家人一切都好。

米拉

---

第一個版本可以說根本發揮不了任何作用，即使葛蘭達得到這個實習機會，也不會是因為她的導師所寫的這封信。這封信的作者無禮（暗示記者的工作不受重視）、白目（承認自己已經將報紙退訂），而且還非常傲慢（因為自己「逢人就推薦」這份報紙，以及介紹了這位「一流」的實習生，而表現得一副施恩於收件人的樣子，還假定葛蘭達一定會獲得這份工作）。

第二個版本則因其謙遜、**以對方為主**、設身處地為對方著想（告訴他"No pressure here"「不要有壓力」），以及不過分恭維（"I know you've been a mentor to many"「我知道你指導過很多實習生」）的態度，而可望發揮預期的效果。此版本雖然比第一個版本略長，但更快切入重點，且只提供有用的資訊。如果葛蘭達真的有潛力，在這個版本的推薦之下，她很有希望獲得面試的機會，並有可能得到這份實習工作。

有時，為了讓犯錯的員工清楚了解自己的錯誤，以及／或是為了留下紀錄，你可能必須透過電子郵件訓誡員工。試比較以下兩個正反範例，看看若員工寄了一封具冒犯性的電子郵件給所有組員，可以如何處理：

**✕ 錯誤示範：**

Subject: You Are in Trouble

Ted—

What on earth were you thinking when you sent that "joke"? Your coworkers sure didn't appreciate it one bit, and neither did I. Don't tell me it was "just a joke." Haven't you cracked your employee handbook and read our company's policies? You've never done this before, that I am aware of. Don't ever send an e-mail like this one again.

Bill Morton
Office Manager

主旨：你麻煩大了

泰德：

當你寄出那封「笑話」時，你的腦袋到底在想什麼？同事們顯然一點也不欣賞那個笑話，我也一樣。別跟我說「這只是個笑話」。你沒看過員工手冊，讀過公司的政策嗎？就我所知，你以前沒犯過這樣的錯，以後請不要再寄像這樣的電子郵件。

比爾摩頓
辦公室經理

## ○ 正確示範：

Subject: Disruption Caused by Your E-mail

Ted—

What one person considers funny, another may find offensive and insulting. Several people have complained to me about the e-mail headed "Have You Heard This One" that you sent everyone yesterday. I was as upset as they were by the foul language, which is inappropriate for an e-mail sent at work. Our company's policy does not make an exception for offensive language, even when used in jest. Please think about how future e-mails will affect your coworkers. If I receive complaints again, HR will have to get involved. But I trust that won't be necessary.

Bill

主旨：你的電子郵件引起的騷動

泰德：

有些人覺得好笑的笑話，其他人可能覺得具有冒犯性和侮辱性。好幾個人向我抱怨你昨天寄給大家那封標題為「聽過這個笑話嗎」的電子郵件。對於信中粗俗的言語，我和他們一樣不悅，這些用語實在不適合出現在工作場合寄送的電子郵件。即使只是個笑話，但公司政策不會為冒犯性言語破例。請你想想日後的電子郵件對其他同仁會有什麼影響。如果再有人向我抱怨，我就必須請人力資源部門介入處理，但我相信不會有這個必要。

比爾

在第一版信件中，很清楚能看出作者的怒氣，而這大概也是這封信唯一清楚的地方。泰德一定既覺得自己蠢（“What on earth were you thinking”「你的腦袋到底在想什麼」和“Haven't you cracked your employee handbook”「你沒看過員工手冊嗎」），又感到害怕（“Don't ever”「再也不要」），但作者卻未說明泰德是哪裡做錯及為什麼做錯，而泰德也不太可能敢開口問（“Don't tell me it was 'just a joke'”「別跟我說『這只是個笑話』」）。

第二封信的口氣則不會讓收件人馬上產生防禦心理。這次作者明確指出問題的根源（“the e-mail headed 'Have You Heard This One' that you sent every one yesterday”「你昨天寄給大家那封標題為『聽過這個笑話嗎』的電子郵件」），並說明該信件所造成的影響、違反的規定及相關後果。這回泰德應該比較能理解自己所犯的錯誤。

## 重點回顧

- 說話不要拐彎抹角，並注意維持有禮的語氣。在開頭二到三句話之內，就要說明寫這封信的重點。
- 在沒有先檢查過收件人名單之前，絕對不要點擊「回覆所有人」，只要把信寄給需要知道內容的人就好。
- 信件內容應盡可能簡短。將信件限制在單一顯示畫面可看完的長度，保持內容精簡切題，讓收件人能快速掌握重點。
- 透過簡潔的主旨讓收件人知道你寫這封信的原因，以及對他們有何意義。如果他們需要採取任何動作，也應在主旨明確說明。
- 不要為了偷懶而忽略寫作的標準慣例，就算是用拇指在行動裝置上打字，也別因此懈怠。

• NOTE •

第 19 章

# 商業信件
Business Letters

商業信件並不是舊時代的古董。無論是要糾正合作廠商的錯誤、推薦適合某職缺的人選，或公告新的服務，各式各樣的情況都必須透過商業信件來達成目的。商業信件若寫得好，可協助提高獲利，比方說取得重要客戶續簽大筆訂單，或是透過長期合作，說服服務供應商降低收費。此外，商業信件也有助於建立商譽，進而可能帶來財務上的回報。

本章所指出的重點正可協助你取得以上各種成果。

## 使用直接親切的用語

你常會在信件中看到enclosed please find（請查收附件）和as per（按照、依據）等公式化用語。這類詞彙聽起來厲害，實際上卻沒什麼成效。捨棄這些用語，可以讓你的信讀起來更清楚、更吸引人。

## 把信寫得清楚、有說服力的祕訣

- **以目標讀者為中心。**試著少以I開頭，可以的話多用you（例如："You were so kind to..."您太客氣了…、"You might be interested..."你可能會對…有興趣」）。把收件人擺在最重要的位置，因為，老實說，只有這樣才能抓住對方的興趣。不要說"I just thought I'd drop you a note to say that I really enjoyed my time as your guest last week."（我只是想寫個便條告訴你，上週到你家作客真的很開心。），可改寫成："What a wonderful host you were last week."（你上週真是個稱職的好主人。）
- **說點有意義的內容。**確保訊息簡短扼要，但具有實質內容，而不僅僅是空泛的話語。不要說"I trust this finds you prospering in business, thriving in your personal life, and continuing to seek the wisdom that will bring lasting satisfaction in all your dealings."（我相信這件事之後，你一定可生意興旺，生活美滿，並可繼續尋求智慧，讓你的所有業務都長長久久，圓圓滿滿。），可改寫成"I hope you and your family and friends all dodged the fires last week in Maniton Springs—which sounded devastating."（上週發生在曼尼頓溫泉的大火聽說非常嚴重，希望你和你的家人朋友都平安躲過了那場

大火。）

- **避免模稜兩可，含糊其辭。**不要說“It is with regret that we acknowledge that we do not appear at this time to be in a position to extend an offer of employment.”（很抱歉，我們確認了目前似乎沒有徵人的打算。），可改寫成：“We're sorry to say that we aren't now hiring.”（很抱歉，我們目前沒有在徵人。）

| ✕ 錯誤示範： | ○ 正確示範： |
|---|---|
| Enclosed please find...<br>請參見附件… | Here are... ; Enclosed are...<br>以下是…；附上… |
| As per your request...<br>依照您的要求… | As you requested...<br>你所要求的… |
| We are in receipt of...<br>我方已收到… | We've received...<br>我們已收到… |
| We shall advise you...<br>我們會告知您… | We'll let you know...<br>我們會通知你… |
| As per your letter...<br>如您信中所說… | As your letter notes...<br>依你信中提到的… |

| | |
|---|---|
| We have your order and will transmit same...<br>我們已收到您的訂單並將代為傳送… | We'll forward your order promptly...<br>我們會立即轉交你的訂單… |
| We take pleasure...<br>我們深感榮幸… | We're glad...<br>我們很高興… |
| Due to the fact that...<br>基於以下緣故… | Because...<br>因為… |
| At an early date...<br>最早的日期… | Soon...<br>盡快… |
| In respect of the matter of...<br>就…而言 | Regarding...<br>關於… |

很多人在對所寫的訊息感到尷尬不安時，常會把信寫得又臭又長，用上各種生硬冗長的用詞。試想想以下兩則範例有何不同。第一封信是飯店經理寫給房客的歡迎信，第二封是我改寫的版本。

**✕ 錯誤示範：**

Dear Valued Guest:

Welcome to the Milford Hotel Santa Clara. We are delighted that you have selected our hotel during the time when you will be here in the Silicon Valley area. Our staff is ready to assist you in any way and ensure that your stay here is an enjoyable and excellent one in every way.

During your time here at the Milford Hotel Santa Clara, we would like to inform you that the hotel is installing new toilet facilities in all guest rooms. This project will begin on Tuesday, May 8 until Tuesday, May 29. The project engineers will begin at 9:00 a.m. and conclude for the day at 5:30 p.m. The team of associates will begin work on the 14th floor and will work in descending order until completion. During these hours, you may see the new or old toilets in the guest room corridors during the exchange process, and we will ensure that a high level of cleanliness standards will be upheld. We think you'll soon appreciate fresh toilet seats. Should you be in your guest room during the toilet exchange and/or wish not to be disturbed, we recommend that you please utilize your Do Not Disturb sign by placing it on the handle of your guest room door.

The vending area should remain sanitary, so feel free to have a candy bar or beverage of your preference. For your convenience, there are safes located in the bottom nightstand drawer in your guest room to safely store your valuables. There may also be available to you utilization of our safe deposit boxes located at the Front Desk.

We appreciate your cooperation and understanding while we continue to improve the delivery system and appearance of our guest room product. Our goal is to minimize any inconvenience related to the toilet-exchange project. Please contact our Manager on Duty should you have any questions or concerns. Once again, please be assured of our utmost devotion to the total quality of your stay within the confines of the Milford Hotel Santa Clara.

On behalf of myself and all the other management personnel and staff of employees here, we wish to reiterate our thanks for your selection and confidence that each and every factor of your stay here will be more than satisfactory.

Sincerely,

[386字]

尊敬的顧客，您好：

歡迎光臨聖塔克拉拉米爾福德飯店。很高興您在來到矽谷地區的這段時間選擇入住本飯店，我們的員工已準備好以任何方式為您提供協助，確保在各方面給您一段愉快、絕佳的住宿體驗。

在您入住聖塔克拉拉米爾福德飯店的這段期間，我們要通知您本飯店正在為每間客房安裝新的馬桶設施。安裝工程將於5月8日星期二開始，直到5月29日星期二結束。工程人員會於早上九點開始作業，於下午五點三十分結束。相關團隊會自十四樓開始施工，逐層往下直至完工。在施工時段，您可能會在更換設施期間，在客房走廊看到新舊馬桶，但我們保證會採取最高水準的清潔標準。相信很快您就會因為嶄新的馬桶座而感到欣喜。若您在更換馬桶時待在客房內，或您不想被人打擾，建議您請多加善用「請勿打擾」標誌，將標誌掛在房門手把上。

販賣區理應會維持整潔，所以您可在此享用喜歡的糖果棒或飲料。為方便您使用，客房內床頭櫃最底層的抽屜都設有保險箱，可供您安全存放貴重物品。飯店前台也設有保管箱可讓您加以利用。

在我們持續改善設施提供和客房外觀的同時，感謝您的配合及理解。我們的目標是盡可能減少因馬桶更換作業所造成的不便。如果您有任何問題或疑慮，請與我們的值班經理聯絡。再次向您保證，在您下榻聖塔克拉拉米爾福德飯店期間，我們會竭誠提供最佳服務品質。謹代表我個人及本飯店其他所有管理人員和員工，再次感謝您選擇入住，並保證在本飯店住宿期間，各方面絕對都能讓您滿意。

謹啟

**○ 正確示範：**

Dear Valued Guest:

Welcome to the Milford Hotel Santa Clara. We're delighted you're staying here, and we're ready to help make your stay both enjoyable and productive.

This month, we're renovating the bathrooms, starting with the 14th floor and working our way down. Although you may have occasion to see or hear workers (during the day), we're striving to minimize disruptions.

Always feel free to use your "Do Not Disturb" sign while you're in your room to ensure that our staff will respect your privacy. And if the renovations ever become a nuisance, please call me (extension 4505): I'll see what I can do. The renovations are but one example of our commitment to providing first-rate lodging.

Thank you again for joining us.

Sincerely,

[125字]

尊敬的顧客，您好：

歡迎光臨聖塔克拉拉米爾福德飯店。很高興您選擇入住本飯店，我們已準備好提供您愉快又充實的住宿體驗。

這個月，我們的浴室正在整修，從十四樓開始逐層往下。雖然您可能會看到工人或聽到他們的聲音（白天時），但我們會盡可能減少干擾。

當您待在房間時，您隨時可使用「請勿打擾」標誌，以確保服務人員不會侵犯到您的隱私。如果整修作業對您造成不便，請致電告知（分機4505），我會竭誠為您服務。此整修作業和其他改善事項，都是為了實踐我們提供一流住宿品質的承諾。

再次謝謝您的入住。

謹啟

---

原本的那封信用字累贅（以guest room product來表示「客房」），重複性高（toilet出現了五次），言辭誇張（excellent... in every way稱自家飯店「在各方面都極出色」），語氣官僚（there may also be available to you utilization「可讓您加以利用」），細節清楚到令人不悅（告訴房客「you may see the new or old toilets 可能會看到新舊馬桶」），甚至令人噁心（在說完新舊馬桶後，緊接著提到可以「have a candy bar 享用糖果棒」）。這樣的寫法似乎註定會引人反感，讓願意花時間看信的房客打退堂鼓。相較之下，修改後的版本傳達溫暖和貼心的態度，並以「你」為主體。

盡快進入重點，以最簡單的方式表達要說的內容。想想奧運的跳水比賽：乾淨俐落的入水，不濺起水花，隨即迅速的出水上岸。若你是以公司的名義寫信，可用we來指稱公司。比起使用被動語態，（It has been decided相較於We have decided），或使用沒有人情味的第三人稱（this organization相較於we），用we給人較溫暖親切的感覺。試想想以下兩者的差別：

| ✕ 錯誤示範： | ○ 正確示範： |
| --- | --- |
| The Mercantile Association of Greater Gotham is delighted to count you among its newest members. The Mercantile Association will provide not only networking opportunities but also advantageous insurance rates, concierge services, and Internet advertising to its members. If you ever confront business issues with which the Mercantile Association might be able to devote its resources, it stands ready to be of assistance.<br><br>大高譚地區商會很高興歡迎你加入成為最新會員。本商會不僅提供建立人脈的機會，更提供會員優惠的保險費率、禮賓服務和網路廣告。如果你遇到任何業務問題，本商會將竭盡資源，隨時準備好提供協助。 | Here at the Mercantile Association of Greater Gotham, we're delighted to count you among our newest members. We provide not only networking opportunities but also advantageous insurance rates, concierge services, and Internet advertising. If you ever confront business issues we can help with, we'll do whatever we can. Just let us know.<br><br>在大高譚地區商會，我們很高興歡迎你加入成為最新會員。我們不僅提供建立人脈的機會，更提供優惠的保險費率、禮賓服務和網路廣告。如果你遇到任何業務問題，而我們正好可提供協助，只要告訴我們，我們也會竭誠為你服務。 |

在左邊的範例中，使用被動語態（is delighted）和重複提及機構名稱（出現在每一句），使作者和目標讀者之間產生了距離感，讓這

封信讀起來像是封廣告或推銷信。右邊的版本則用了you和we來營造歸屬感和人際間的連結。

## 激勵目標讀者採取行動

商業信件必須符合讀者的需求，才能取得預期成果。說得出能讓他們在乎的原因，他們才會採取行動。

為非營利組織請求募款是最難寫的信件類型之一，想想若是你會如何寫。下筆的關鍵得先了解一般人捐款給慈善機構的原因。雖然行銷人員常引用恐懼、內疚、獨特性、貪婪、憤怒、救贖和讚美等七項「基本動機」來解釋消費者的反應，但實際情況卻有更細微的差別。可成功激勵對方響應你的請求而慷慨解囊，通常是基於以下八個主要原因：

- 他們相信自己的捐款可帶來影響。
- 他們相信你的機構所代表的價值。
- 捐款可讓他們獲得讚許和肯定。
- 認為自己可與名人或受尊敬的人搭上關係。
- 可提高歸屬感，認為自己是令人尊敬的團體中的一分子。
- 可排解恐懼和內疚等負面情緒。
- 他們認為這是應盡的責任。
- 可享有節稅的好處。

撰寫募款信的某些原則就是從這些捐款原因衍生而來，因此一封成功的募款信必須：(1)直接針對個人提出請求；(2)描繪一個願景，讓收件人可藉由支持一個值得努力的目標，來滿足個人需求；以及(3)促使收件人採取具體果決的行動。（這些原則也適用於其他類型的商業信件。）

來看看上述理論如何實際應用在募款信件中：

Dear Marion:

May I count you in as a table sponsor at the Annual Dinner of the Tascosa Children's Home of North Texas? Your sponsorship will pay a month's room and board for one of the 50 orphaned teenagers that we care for.

The event will be held at 6:00 p.m. on July 1 at Snowdon Country Club, and the emcee will be the nationally syndicated television host Spooner Hudson—our longtime national spokesperson. Celebrity chef Margrit Lafleur promises to serve up one of his memorable dinners, and the wines will be personally selected by master sommelier Peter Brunswick. Most excitingly, two mystery guests from Beverly Hills will be there that evening—among the best-known philanthropists in the world.

As a table sponsor, you'll be credited as one of our Patron Angels—and, believe me, the tangible gratitude of our kids will bring you the lasting satisfaction that you have vastly improved their lives and well-being. Our kids are reachable and teachable, but only through the generosity of our community's philanthropic leaders.

Many people, of course, can't help us in our mission. We count on our Patron Angels. I hope you'll spend a few minutes browsing through the Home's brochure (enclosed) and that you'll fill out the card committing to fill ten seats at your table (a $1,500 tax-deductible gift).

I look forward to hearing from you soon.

Sincerely,

親愛的瑪麗恩：

北德州的塔斯科薩兒童之家即將舉辦年度晚宴，我可以算你一份加入晚宴贊助的行列嗎？有了你的贊助，就可為我們照顧的五十位失親青少年中的一位，支付一個月的食宿費用。

晚宴將於七月一日晚上六點在斯諾登鄉村俱樂部舉行，由全國聯播的電視節目主持人斯普納哈德遜主持，他也是我們長期以來的全國發言人。名廚馬格里特拉弗爾承諾將會送上一頓令人難忘的晚餐，搭配的酒則會由侍酒大師彼得布朗斯維克親自挑選。最讓人興奮的是，當天晚上還會有兩位來自比佛利山的神祕嘉賓，兩位都是全球最著名的慈善家。

如果贊助晚宴，你將可獲得我們的「贊助天使」頭銜，而且，相信我，孩子們的實質感謝會讓滿足感長期縈繞在你的心中，因為你的慷慨解囊大幅改善了孩子的生活和健康。我們的孩子可以學習和成長，都是透過社區中慈善領導者的慷慨捐助才得以實現。

當然，有許多人無法協助我們達成使命，因此我們得仰賴贊助天使。希望你能花幾分鐘瀏覽兒童之家的手冊（已隨信附上），並填寫願意在你的桌次贊助十個座位的卡片（可減稅 $1,500 美元的禮卡）。

希望能很快收到你的回覆。

謹啟

現在，再回頭看看在給瑪麗恩（我們虛構的收件人）的這封信之前所列出的八點原因，作者將每一點都寫進了這封信中。像這樣的一封信，應該可望吸引不少收件人立即採取行動。

## 緩和壞消息的衝擊

若要在信中拒絕別人，可採用「三明治溝通法」，將拒絕的話夾在令人開心的話之間，不要劈頭就說「不」。**開頭先說些真誠肯定的話，再解釋決定拒絕的原因，這樣目標讀者會比較能承受被拒絕的失望**，也較有可能在自己的要求遭拒後，仍達成你的希望，例如購買商品、報名網路研討會、續訂會員等。

| ✕ 錯誤示範： | ○ 正確示範： |
| --- | --- |
| We regret to inform you that we cannot supply the 500 copies of Negotiate It Now! at the 60% discount that you have requested. No one—not even one of our authors, and not even the biggest bookselling chains—receives such a hefty discount. If you would care to resubmit your order at the more modest figure of 30%, we will gladly consider the order at that time. But I can offer no guarantees.<br><br>很抱歉通知你，我們無法以你要求的四折價格提供500本《談判技巧立即上手！》。即使是我們的作者或規模最大的連鎖書店，都無法獲 | How rewarding to hear that you intend to use Negotiate It Now! as part of your business summit. You've chosen the best book on the subject, and we'd be delighted to supply it. Although you've requested a 60% discount off list price, the most we can offer is 30%. That's the largest discount available to anyone, and we're happy to extend it to you with a purchase of 500 copies.<br><br>很榮幸聽到你想要在商業高峰會中使用《談判技巧立即上手！》這本書。你的選擇絕對是這類主題書籍的首選，我們很高興能為你提供此書。 |

| | |
|---|---|
| 得如此低的折扣。如果你願意以較合理的七折價格重新訂購，我們會很樂意考慮接受你的訂單，但並不保證結果。 | 雖然你要求定價的四折優惠，但我們最多只能打七折。這是我們所能給予的最低折扣，我們也很樂意為你訂購的500本書提供此優惠。 |

雖然無論怎麼說，接獲壞消息的人可能都還是會不開心，但在某個程度上，你可稍微掌控讓他們不致太過不悅。以下提供一些小祕訣：

- 從目標讀者的角度思考，拿出你最好的態度。若對方表現無禮，你仍應以禮待之；若對方態度焦躁，試著理解；若對方仍有疑惑，清楚告知；若對方堅持己見，耐心安撫；若對方願意配合，誠心致謝；若對方指責抱怨，保持理性、公正的態度，承認任何過失。
- 直接回答問題。
- 不用過度解釋，只須說明要傳達的重點。
- 盡可能簡單說明，不要用「業界行話」或商務術語。
- 使用體貼、有人情味的語氣，不要像機器人般冷冰冰。

即使你在信中應允對方的要求或給予好處，但若語意不清、口氣勉強，或對目標讀者的問題漠不關心，仍有可能會惹惱收件人。

**✕ 錯誤示範：**

Joan—

In response to your request for a travel subsidy to the conference where your award will be given, Jonathan has reminded me of our current discretionary-spending freeze. He has decided, however, to make an exception in this instance so long as your flight is no more than $400 and you stick to a $50 per diem. Please submit your fully documented expenses upon your return.

Sincerely,

Rebekah

瓊恩：

針對你所要求出席會議領獎的差旅補助，喬納森跟我提到了目前的裁量性支出凍結。然而，他還是決定對這件事情破例，前提是機票費用不可超過$400美元，每日開銷不超過$50美元。請在回來後，立即提交所有費用明細。

謹啟

雷貝卡

**○ 正確示範：**

Joan—

Congratulations on your Spivey Award! We're delighted for you. Jonathan hastened to tell me that despite our current discretionary-spending freeze, he wants to support your travel to accept your award. We can manage a $400 flight reimbursement and a $50 per diem for on-the-ground expenses. You'll be a great company representative, I know, and I only wish I could be there myself to see you honored.

Sincerely,

Rebekah

瓊恩：

恭喜你獲得斯皮維獎！我們都很為你高興。喬納森迫不及待的來跟我說，雖然我們目前凍結裁量性支出，但他還是想支持你前往領獎。我們可撥出$400美元的機票報銷費用，以及每天$50美元的日常開銷。我知道，你會很完美的代表公司，真希望能親眼看到你領獎。

謹啟

雷貝卡

Brandy—

At this time you have now used up all your available sick-leave days and vacation days for the year. A sister-in-law does not qualify for the closeness of relation required for an employee to be eligible for compensated bereavement leave, so you will be docked for any days you choose to be absent next week around the time of the funeral. I'm afraid that policy is simply inflexible, and I checked with Jane to confirm this.

Sincerely,

Pamela

Brandy—

Once again I want to extend my condolences for your family's loss. Take the time you need next week to be with your family. I'm sorry to report that the days will be uncompensated, according to our policies for bereavement leave, but I hope you'll call on me if I can do anything else for you in this time of need. Jane joins me in sending our heartfelt sympathies.

Sincerely,

Pamela

布蘭迪：

目前，你已用完今年所有可用的病假和年假。與嫂嫂的親屬關係不符合可請有薪喪假的資格，因此下週你在葬禮前後所請的假會列為扣薪假。關於這點我已經與珍確認過，但相關規定就是這樣。

謹啟

潘蜜拉

布蘭迪：

我要再次對你的家人失去至親致上深切的慰問之意。下週你可以請假，好好陪伴你的家人。但我必須很遺憾的告訴你，根據我們的喪假規定，這幾天假是不給薪的假。但如果有其他任何我能在這種時刻為你做的事，請儘管開口。珍和我一同向你表達我們最真摯的慰問。

謹啟

潘蜜拉

## 請參見隨附內容
## （Enclosed Please Find）

看看長期以來，其他商業寫作者對於這類生硬的用語有何看法：

**理查德格蘭特懷特（Richard Grant White, 1880）：**「在我看來，沒有比Please find enclosed更荒謬的用詞了。」

**舒爾文科迪（Sherwin Cody, 1908）：**「任何你在說話時不會用的刻板字詞，在寫信時也都應該避免。有些人認為，商業信件就是要用某些奇特的商務術語才恰當，但事實上，正是這些只在商業信件才會看到的特殊用字，對業務帶來的傷害最深。若要測試某個字詞或表達方式是否適當，可以問問自己『如果不是寫信，而是直接和顧客說話，我會這麼說嗎？』」

**華萊士E.巴塞洛繆（Wallace E. Bartholomew）和弗洛伊德赫爾伯特（Floyd Hurlbut）（1924）：**「在Inclosed herewith please find（隨函覆上）這個用語中，Inclosed和herewith是一樣的意思。向對方重複兩次支票的位置，還建議要他們找一找，實在有夠蠢，其實只要說“We are inclosing our check for $25.50”（我們已附上 $25.50 美元的支票）就行了。」

**A.查爾斯貝本若斯（A. Charles Babenroth, 1942）：**「Enclosed please find 是個無用且錯誤的用語。在這個例子中，

please這個字幾乎毫無意義，find 這個字也用得不恰當。Enclosed please find sample of our #1939 black elastic ribbon.（請參見隨附編號1939的黑色鬆緊帶樣本。）是不好的寫法，建議改寫成：We are enclosing（或We enclose）a sample of our #1939 black elastic ribbon.」（我們已附上編號1939的黑色鬆緊帶樣本。）

**L.E.佛萊利(L. E. Frailey, 1965)：**「在商業信件中，太常看到太多像enclosed herewith、enclosed please find、herewith please find等千篇一律的老套用語，要說這些詞彙是陳腔濫調或老生常談都好，隨你怎麼說都行。它們就像是安眠藥讓人昏昏欲睡，完全違背了寫信與收件人溫馨親切交流的目標。」

**傑拉德J.阿爾德(Gerald J. Alred)、查爾斯T.布魯索(Charles T. Brusaw)和沃爾特E.奧利烏(Walter E. Oliu)(1993)：**「不必要的使用太正式的字眼（例如herewith）和過時的用語（例如please find enclosed），是令人感覺做作的另一個原因。」

**凱利卡農(Kelly Cannon, 2004)：**「對商業信件來說，有些原則是放諸四海皆準的。例如“Inure to the benefit of（對…有益處）”，除了benefit以外，另外四個字皆為贅字；“enclosed please find”聽起來浮誇又愚蠢；“I am writing this letter to inform you that...”則是一句無腦的廢話。」

## 不要在憤怒的情緒下寫信

學會善良和圓融，多說請和謝謝。在任何商業往來中，都必須保持謙恭有禮的態度，即使是寫抱怨信也不例外。若言行無禮，會讓你成為別人眼中難相處的怪人。保持禮貌同時仍可有話直說，兩者並不衝突。

**✕ 錯誤示範：**

We are astonished at your complaint. The brochures that we printed were exactly as you specified. You okayed the sample paper, the typesetting, and the proofreading (we gave you an extra three hours). You chose the hot-pink borders with the fine-screen halftones in the body type against our advice. You insisted on drop-shipping by the 18th, and as you know, a rushed job does not allow for first-rate press work. Moreover, we quoted you a bargain-basement price. Under the circumstances we believe that any unbiased observer would say that we performed remarkably well under the impossible conditions you imposed.

對於你們的投訴，我們感到非常震驚，這份手冊完全是依你們的指示印刷。從樣張、排版到校對（我們還多給你們三小時的時間），你們

**○ 正確示範：**

We agree with you that the brochures did not match the high standards you have a right to expect from us. But we believed, in this instance, that you considered the color quality less crucial than a low price and a quick turnaround. So we pushed the work through production in three days' less time than we usually require. We advised against your using hot-pink borders and fine-screen halftones on the grade of paper you chose. Still, we exercised some ingenuity to achieve better results than are ordinarily possible. I mention this not to avoid responsibility but merely to suggest that we did the best that could be done under difficult circumstances. If you'll allow us a few more days next time, as you ordinarily do, the results will be better.

都確認過沒問題。你們罔顧我們的建議，執意選擇在正文部分使用亮粉色邊框和細網版半色調印刷，且堅持在十八日之前發貨，但你也知道，趕工出不了細活。此外，我們的報價是最便宜的價格。在這種情況下，我相信在任何不帶偏見的人看來，都會認為在你們施加的各種不可能的條件下，我們已經做得非常好。

我們同意手冊品質並不符合你們有權期望我們達到的高標準，但在此案例中，我們認為你們對低價和快速完工的重視，更勝於對色彩品質的要求。因此，我們加緊在三天內趕工，所花的時間比平常來得少。我們也曾提過不建議在你們所選的紙質上，使用亮粉色邊框和細網版半色調印刷，但我們仍運用了一些巧思，達到比一般情況下更好的成果。我提這些並不是要推卸責任，只是想表達我們已盡力在不利的情況下做到最好。如果下次你們能和平常一樣，多給我們幾天時間，成果一定會更好。

---

如你所見，用像要吵架的高傲語氣說話，除了會激怒和疏遠目標讀者，可能還會讓你失去一位客戶。另一種較圓融的方式，一樣傳達了重點（趕工的代價就是無法兼顧品質），但卻不會打壞關係。

當你收到不講道理的信時，別想著要以牙還牙，這樣只會開啟一連串負面的連鎖反應。以致力提供一流服務的心態來處理抱怨信，拿出與面對面溝通時同樣溫暖友善的態度來寫信。如果錯在你或你的公司，不要試圖忽略、掩蓋或推卸責任。這麼做不但無法騙過對方，反而會火上加油，使對方更生氣。當你犯了錯，勇於認錯，說明你做了什麼（或將會做什麼）來改正錯誤，並強調會盡力改善服務。

### 重點回顧

- 使用簡單、親近、直接的文字，避免沒有實質意義，只會讓信件讀來浮誇冗長的制式用語。
- 舉出能讓目標讀者重視的原因，以激勵對方在看過信後採取行動。
- 傳達負面的訊息時，開頭先提正面的消息，以緩和帶來的衝擊。接著再說明造成該結果的原因，但無須過度解釋。
- 站在目標讀者的立場，保持禮貌、有同情心、專業的態度。
- 保持禮貌圓融的態度。若犯了任何錯誤，應勇於承擔責任。

## • NOTE •

第 20 章

# 備忘錄和報告

Memos and Reports

備忘錄和報告常見的功用不外乎兩個，一是讓目標讀者了解問題的最新情況，二是促使讀者採取行動，有時則還須同時兼顧兩者。因此，從標題、摘要、正文到結論，每個部分都必須清清楚楚，讓讀者能立即掌握你要傳達的資訊和事項。

## 選擇簡短清晰的標題

無論是備忘錄主旨或報告的標題，都必須選擇簡潔穩妥的用字，確切說明文件的內容。

| ✕ 錯誤示範： | ○ 正確示範： |
|---|---|
| Subject: Siegelson<br>主旨：Siegelson | Subject: Approval of Siegelson Acquisition<br>主旨：核准 Siegelson 收購案 |

| | |
|---|---|
| Subject: Settlement<br>主旨：和解 | Subject: Why We Should Reject Frost's Settlement Offer<br>主旨：為什麼應拒絕Frost的和解提議 |
| Subject: Print Run<br>主旨：印刷數量 | Subject: Ginsburg Autobiography Print Run<br>主旨：金斯堡自傳印刷數量 |

左邊列出的標題對所涵蓋的主題只是點到即止，目標讀者對於自己該做什麼還是一無所知。右邊的標題則較為明確（也不會太冗長）：第一個和第三個標題說明了最新狀態，第二個標題則是要求讀者遵循建議。

## 在開頭總結主要重點摘要

決定好你打算要處理幾個問題，建議最好不超過三個（請參見第4章），接著針對每個問題：(1)以任何人都能理解的方式說明問題，(2)提出你的解決辦法，以及(3)說明提出此解決辦法的原因。以下提供一則範例：

**Summary**

**Issue:** Arnold Paper Supply has consistently failed to meet our deadlines for delivery of multicolor, printed cardstock.

**Proposed Solution:** Switch to National Paper and Plastics

Company, which has a higher fixed fee.

**Reason:** Though National Paper and Plastics Company has a higher rate per delivery, its turnaround is quicker. This will increase efficiency in the warehouse, allow us to fill more orders, and help us to establish goodwill with retailers who have been angry with us for not meeting their deadlines.

**摘要**

**問題：**阿諾德紙業公司經常延誤彩色印刷卡紙的交期期限。

**建議的解決方案：**改與全國製紙和塑膠公司合作，雖然他們的固定費用較高。

**原因：**雖然全國製紙和塑膠公司的每次交貨費用較高，但他們的交貨時間較快。這樣一來，可提高我們的倉儲效率，讓我們能履行更多訂單，也能協助我們在零售商之間建立良好商譽。由於我們未能準時交貨，已經惹毛部分廠商。

在文件一開頭就點出所有要點，雖然之後得將一樣的內容再複述一次，但這麼做是為了強化觀點，並不會顯得多餘。目標讀者可從一開始的簡短介紹快速掌握大方向，而後完整說明的正文部分則會一一詳述各個重點，並提供可作為佐證的細節和資料。建議你在撰寫第一版初稿時，可來回參照摘要和正文：先在摘要中說明問題，並提供你能提出最好的解決辦法；隨著備忘錄或報告的正文漸有進展後，再回頭修改摘要的問題和解決辦法。

摘要內容是為了三種目標讀者而寫：

- 這類讀者以高階主管為主，他們只有興趣快速了解最新情況、你對此問題的研究和結論，或是相關建議。
- 這類讀者可能會被找來（在你知情或不知情的情況下）評估你的文件是否完善，並根據他們所做的事實查證和批判性分析，評斷此文件的好壞。
- 也許在你寫完文件一段時間之後，未來的讀者（包括兩年後成為第一類高階主管的讀者）必須從你的文件發掘有用的資訊。（畢竟，備忘錄和報告很少會立即付諸實行：這類文件通常會被擱置一旁，短則幾週到幾個月，長則甚至可達數年，直到有人取得資源，或接到命令，才有得以實行的一天。）

這三類目標讀者理應都該獲得你的關注。更重要的是，如果你希望你建議的事項能有任何進展，你必須要能說服他們。

即使要探究的問題是別人所指派給你，你也必須在摘要中對問題加以定義。

## 撰寫報告時…

- 確保你了解撰寫報告的原因和要報告的內容。
- 根據自己的背景知識和初期所做的研究，盡你所能寫好摘要，簡要的陳述問題和解決方法，並說明此方法為何有效或為何優於其他方法。

- 識別相關資料的來源。
- 從這些來源中，盡可能收集所有資料和說明。
- 整理相關的觀察和推論資料，捨棄其餘不相關的部分。
- 彙整研究結果，以報告的形式呈現。
- 根據正文修改摘要內容。

身為作者，你是最有資格限定報告範圍的人：指派你做報告的人不見得能充分了解問題，因此未必能夠正確的提問，或能了解原來這個問題還包含三個子問題。

事實上，你也是在做了研究之後才清楚這些細節，例如你可能去挖掘資料以找出潛藏的問題所在，或查閱文件參考其他組織如何解決類似問題，或是與曾找出實用解決辦法的人一起討論。想要了解問題，你必須做足功課，然後才能清楚的說明問題，讓所有人都理解為何有解決此問題的必要。

如果要提出建議，你必須說明：(1)必須執行的事項，(2)由誰負責執行，(3)執行的時間和地點，(4)必須執行的原因，以及(5)該如何執行。

以下是一份簡短的行銷報告範例：

**Marketing Strategy for Skinny Mini Line of Chocolates**

## Summary

**Issue:** Within the last fiscal year, Pantheon Chocolate's sales have dropped from $13,320,000 to $10,730,000, but its market share remains unchanged at 37%.

**Proposed Solution:** Increase promotion of the Skinny Mini line of chocolates. These chocolates contain less sugar and fat than the regular line.

**Reason:** Health-conscious consumers want low-calorie options but don't want to sacrifice full flavor. The Skinny Mini chocolates have fewer calories than Pantheon's regular chocolates but the same flavor.

**Consumers are buying more "healthy alternative" chocolates**

Because consumers increasingly regard sugar and fat as unhealthy, they are not buying as much high-end gourmet chocolate as they were a year ago. This has led to a decline in sales for all high-end chocolate makers, including Pantheon. But for candies marketed as "healthy alternatives" with less sugar and fat and fewer calories, sales have increased 42% in the same period. Marketing studies show that consumers of "healthy alternative" candies are most attracted to low-calorie chocolates that are packaged in specific-calorie portions rather than by weight.

These consumers also complain that low-calorie candies lack the rich flavor that they are used to, and they are willing to pay more for quality. Pantheon already produces a line of low-calorie gourmet chocolates, Skinny Minis, that have fewer calories than Pantheon's regular candies but the same flavor. They're currently sold by the pound or in gift boxes in high-end chocolate boutiques and as elegantly wrapped bars in coffee shops.

**Recommendations**

- To reach more health-conscious consumers, Pantheon should package Skinny Mini chocolates in a variety of portion-controlled sizes and make them available in health-food stores and supermarkets as well as the chocolate and coffee shops.
- The marketing campaign should stress the controlled portion and limited calories of each Skinny Mini bar or gift box, and the packaging should boldly display the low calorie count.

## 纖瘦迷你系列巧克力行銷策略

### 摘要

**問題：** 在上一個會計年度，潘提翁巧克力的銷量從$13,320,000美元下跌至$10,730,000美元，但市占率卻未改變，仍維持在37%。

**建議的解決方案：** 加強宣傳纖瘦迷你系列巧克力，這個系列的含糖量和脂肪均比一般巧克力來得低。

**原因：** 具有健康意識的消費者想要低熱量的選擇，但又不想放棄巧克力的濃醇滋味。纖瘦迷你系列巧克力的熱量比潘提翁旗下一般的巧克力低，但仍保有相同風味。

### 越來越多消費者購買「健康版」的巧克力

由於越來越多的消費者認為糖和脂肪是不健康的東西，因此比起一年前，他們購買高檔精美巧克力的數量減少，使得包括潘提翁在內的所有高檔巧克力製造商的銷量明顯下滑。但在同一期間，標榜低糖低脂低熱量的「健康版」糖果，銷量卻提高了42%。行銷研究顯示，最受購買「健康版」糖果的消費者歡迎的產品，是依特定熱量的份量包裝，而非依重量包裝的低卡巧克力。

這群消費者也抱怨低卡巧克力缺少慣有的濃郁風味，為了品質，他們願意付出更高的價格。潘提翁原就有在出產美味的低卡巧克力「纖瘦迷你系列」，此系列巧克力的熱量比潘提翁一般的產品低，卻能維持相同風味。此系列目前是在高級巧克力精品店，依重量或以禮盒形式販售，或在咖啡店以包裝精美的巧克力棒販售。

**建議**

- 為了觸及更多具有健康意識的消費者，潘提翁應該將纖瘦迷你巧克力的包裝改成不同份量控制的大小，並在健康食品商店和超市以及巧克力和咖啡店販售。
- 行銷活動應著重在強調每份纖瘦迷你巧克力棒或禮盒，其份量均經過精準控制，且每一份的熱量有限，包裝上也應該顯眼的秀出低卡路里含量。

## 重點回顧

- 選擇簡潔的標題或主旨，告訴目標讀者備忘錄或報告所涵蓋的主題，以及他們應採取的行動（或應該要在乎的原因）。
- 在文件一開始先點出重點，並概要說明問題、解決方法和選擇此方法的原因。
- 以這份摘要作為第一份初稿正文的基礎，據此詳加闡述。
- 根據正文修改摘要，以確保摘要確實反映正文內容。

• NOTE •

第 21 章

# 績效考核表

## Performance Appraisals

填寫績效考核表（或稱為員工評鑑表）不必是一件令人生畏的差事。只要看看自己一年來所做的紀錄，問問他人對你的下屬有何意見反饋，並仔細審閱員工的自我評核，有了這些事先收集到的事實數據，若再加上豐富的評鑑詞彙，撰寫考核評語絕不是件難事。本章的目的就是為了提供一些可隨時取用的實用詞句。

以下評語範例共涵蓋工作上的七個層面：態度、效率、人際關係、判斷力、專業知識、可靠性和溝通技巧，但你可根據要評判的任何特質自行改寫。寫完評語後，再提供可作為佐證的具體實例，例如："When we had several layoffs last June, Lauren remained utterly calm and collected while demonstrating keen sensitivity to those who lost their jobs. She [填入任何值得一提的獨特行為]"（去年六月當我們解僱部分同仁時，蘿倫還是非常沉著冷靜，並對那些失去工作的同事展現出高度的體貼。她…）。

## Attitude 態度

| | |
|---|---|
| **Superb**<br>**優秀** | • shows unwavering commitment<br>表現出堅定不移的投入<br>• always gives maximal effort<br>總是拚盡全力<br>• is always friendly and happy to help<br>總是非常友善且樂於助人<br>• always brings out the best in others<br>總是能引出別人最好的一面 |
| **Good**<br>**良好** | • shows strong commitment<br>表現出強烈決心的投入<br>• usually makes a strong effort<br>通常非常努力<br>• is usually friendly and happy to help<br>通常很友善且樂於助人<br>• usually brings out the best in others<br>通常能引出別人最好的一面 |
| **Acceptable**<br>**尚可** | • shows adequate commitment<br>表現出充分的投入<br>• makes an effort<br>會努力去做<br>• is often friendly and happy to help<br>偶爾會很友善且樂於助人 |

| | |
|---|---|
| | • is often a positive influence on the group<br>偶爾會對團隊有正面影響 |
| **Needs Improvement**<br>**欠佳** | • could show more commitment<br>還可以再更投入<br>• doesn't always make an effort<br>有時不太努力<br>• is sometimes quarrelsome<br>有時會與人爭吵<br>• sometimes creates tension within the group<br>有時會在團隊裡造成緊張氣氛 |
| **Poor**<br>**極差** | • lacks commitment<br>對工作不投入<br>• rarely makes a real effort<br>很少真的努力工作<br>• is quarrelsome and sometimes even hostile<br>好與人爭吵，有時甚至充滿敵意<br>• often creates tension within the group<br>經常在團隊裡造成緊張氣氛 |

## Efficiency 效率

| | |
|---|---|
| **Superb**<br>**優秀** | • never wastes time or effort<br>從來不會浪費時間或精力<br>• delegates effectively<br>能有效的委派工作 |

| | |
|---|---|
| | • always completes tasks on time<br>總能準時完成工作<br>• can manage many projects at a time<br>可一次管理多個專案 |
| **Good**<br>**良好** | • rarely wastes time or effort<br>很少會浪費時間或精力<br>• usually delegates appropriately<br>通常能妥善的委派工作<br>• almost always completes tasks on time<br>幾乎總能準時完成工作<br>• can manage several projects at a time<br>可一次管理幾個專案 |
| **Acceptable**<br>**尚可** | • usually doesn't waste time or effort<br>通常不太會浪費時間或精力<br>• delegates pretty well<br>還算能妥善的委派工作<br>• usually completes tasks on time<br>通常可準時完成工作<br>• can manage more than one project at a time<br>可一次管理一個以上的專案 |
| **Needs Improvement**<br>**欠佳** | • sometimes wastes time and effort<br>有時會浪費時間或精力<br>• tries to do too much without delegating<br>嘗試攬下太多業務，而未委派工作 |

| | |
|---|---|
| | • fails to complete tasks on time<br>無法準時完成工作<br>• cannot manage more than one project at a time<br>無法一次管理一個以上的專案 |
| **Poor**<br>**極差** | • often wastes time and effort<br>時常浪費時間或精力<br>• usually fails to delegate when appropriate<br>通常未能適時的委派工作<br>• can't be counted on to complete tasks on time<br>無法讓人信任可否準時完成工作<br>• struggles to manage even one project at a time<br>即使一次管理一個專案都很勉強 |

## Human relations 人際關係

| | |
|---|---|
| **Superb**<br>**優秀** | • demonstrates keen sensitivity to others and an uncanny ability to understand their needs<br>對他人展現出高度的體貼，且具備可了解他人需求的傑出能力<br>• participates actively and collegially in meetings<br>積極且融洽的參與會議討論<br>• works exceptionally well on teams<br>在團隊合作方面特別出色 |

| | |
|---|---|
| | • relates to customers extremely well<br>能夠完美的理解客戶的問題或需求 |
| **Good**<br>**良好** | • usually demonstrates sensitivity to others<br>通常能展現對他人的體貼<br>• participates effectively in meetings<br>可有效的參與會議討論<br>• works effectively on teams<br>可有效進行團隊合作<br>• relates to customers well<br>能夠很好的理解客戶的問題或需求 |
| **Acceptable**<br>**尚可** | • often demonstrates sensitivity to others<br>偶爾能展現對他人的體貼<br>• participates adequately in meetings<br>可充分的參與會議討論<br>• gets along with fellow team members<br>可與團隊成員和睦相處<br>• relates to customers competently<br>能夠完全理解客戶的問題或需求 |
| **Needs Improvement**<br>**欠佳** | • does not always pick up on interpersonal cues<br>有時無法掌握人際溝通的訊號<br>• sometimes wastes others' time in meetings<br>有時會在會議中浪費別人的時間<br>• is sometimes motivated more by personal goals than by team goals<br>有時著重於個人目標勝過團隊目標 |

| | |
|---|---|
| | • sometimes alienates customers through inattention<br>有時會因為漫不經心而與客戶關係疏遠 |
| **Poor**<br>**極差** | • rarely pays attention to others' reactions<br>很少注意到他人的反應<br>• often wastes others' time in meetings<br>常在會議中浪費別人的時間<br>• does not work well on teams<br>無法與別人團隊合作<br>• often alienates customers with impoliteness and sarcasm<br>常因為無禮、嘲諷的態度而與客戶關係疏遠 |

## Judgment 判斷力

| | |
|---|---|
| **Superb**<br>**優秀** | • makes excellent choices and informed decisions<br>能做出最佳選擇和完善的決策<br>• remains utterly calm and collected even in times of crisis<br>即使面對危機，也能保持沉著冷靜<br>• knows precisely which problems need immediate attention and which ones can wait<br>能夠精準判斷問題的輕重緩急<br>• behaves professionally and appropriately in every situation<br>在任何情況都能保持專業、合宜的行為 |

| | |
|---|---|
| Good<br>良好 | • makes sound choices and reasonable decisions<br>能做出明智選擇和合理的決策<br><br>• remains relatively calm and collected even in times of crisis<br>即使面對危機，也能相對保持沉著冷靜<br><br>• generally knows which problems need immediate attention and which ones can wait<br>通常能夠判斷問題的輕重緩急<br><br>• behaves professionally and appropriately<br>能保持專業、合宜的行為 |
| Acceptable<br>尚可 | • generally makes sound choices and informed decisions<br>通常能做出明智選擇和完善的決策<br><br>• remains mostly calm and collected except in times of crisis<br>除了在面對危機時，大多時候能保持沉著冷靜<br><br>• does a pretty good job distinguishing between problems that need immediate attention and those that can wait<br>還算能夠判斷問題的輕重緩急<br><br>• generally behaves professionally and appropriately<br>通常能保持專業、合宜的行為 |
| Needs Improvement<br>欠佳 | • sometimes makes poor choices and ill-informed decisions<br>有時會做出不當的選擇和偏頗的決策 |

| | |
|---|---|
| | • sometimes lacks the calm and collected demeanor required in high-pressure circumstances<br>有時缺乏在高壓情況下需要的沉著冷靜<br>• often doesn't distinguish between problems that need immediate attention and those that can wait<br>經常無法判斷問題的輕重緩急<br>• sometimes behaves unprofessionally and inappropriately<br>有時會有不專業、不適當的行為 |
| **Poor**<br>**極差** | • often makes poor choices and ill-informed decisions<br>時常會做出不當的選擇和偏頗的決策<br>• often lacks the calm and collected demeanor required in high-pressure circumstances<br>經常缺乏在高壓情況下需要的沉著冷靜<br>• typically fails to distinguish between problems that need immediate attention and those that can wait<br>通常無法判斷問題的輕重緩急<br>• often behaves unprofessionally and inappropriately<br>經常會有不專業、不適當的行為 |

## Knowledge 專業知識

| | |
|---|---|
| **Superb**<br>**優秀** | • is exceptionally well informed about all aspects of the job<br>極為了解工作的各個方面<br>• demonstrates extraordinarily comprehensive knowledge<br>展現出卓越的全方位知識<br>• skillfully handles complex assignments without supervision<br>可嫻熟的完成複雜的工作，無需他人指導<br>• has a comprehensive knowledge of the industry<br>對產業有全盤的了解 |
| **Good**<br>**良好** | • is well informed about key aspects of the job<br>非常了解工作的主要方面<br>• demonstrates thorough knowledge<br>展現出透徹的專業知識<br>• can handle complex assignments with some supervision<br>可在旁人稍加指導下完成複雜的工作<br>• has strong knowledge of the industry<br>對產業有深厚的了解 |
| **Acceptable**<br>**尚可** | • understands the job<br>了解工作的內容 |

| | |
|---|---|
| | • demonstrates adequate knowledge<br>展現出充分的專業知識<br>• can handle moderately complex assignments with supervision<br>可在旁人指導下完成複雜的工作<br>• has an acceptable degree of knowledge of the industry<br>對產業有相當程度的了解 |
| **Needs Improvement**<br>**欠佳** | • doesn't fully understand the job<br>不完全了解工作的內容<br>• demonstrates less than satisfactory knowledge<br>顯示出專業知識稍嫌不足<br>• sometimes mishandles assignments of moderate complexity, even with supervision<br>即使有他人指導，有時仍處理不好中等複雜度的工作<br>• has insufficient knowledge of the industry<br>對產業的了解程度不足 |
| **Poor**<br>**極差** | • is ill-informed about many aspects of the job<br>對工作的許多方面都欠缺了解<br>• demonstrates inadequate knowledge<br>顯示出專業知識不足<br>• mishandles basic assignments<br>處理不好基本的工作<br>• has little knowledge of the industry<br>對產業不甚了解 |

## Reliability 可靠性

| | |
|---|---|
| **Superb**<br>**優秀** | • always meets deadlines<br>總是能準時完成工作<br>• is unfailingly dependable<br>無論何時都絕對可靠<br>• achieves excellent results in urgent situations<br>在急迫的情況下，能交出完美成果<br>• always delivers on promises<br>答應的事一定會做到 |
| **Good**<br>**良好** | • meets deadlines<br>能準時完成工作<br>• is highly dependable<br>非常的可靠<br>• achieves good results in urgent situations<br>在急迫的情況下，能交出理想成果<br>• almost always delivers on promises<br>答應的事幾乎都會做到 |
| **Acceptable**<br>**尚可** | • meets most deadlines<br>多數時候能準時完成工作<br>• is dependable<br>很可靠<br>• achieves acceptable results in urgent situations<br>在急迫的情況下，能交出令人滿意的成果 |

| | |
|---|---|
| | • delivers pretty consistently on promises<br>答應的事大部分會做到 |
| **Poor**<br>**極差** | • often fails to meet important deadlines<br>時常無法準時完成重要工作<br><br>• is rarely dependable<br>大多數時候都不可靠<br><br>• often fails to achieve acceptable results in urgent situations<br>在急迫的情況下，常無法交出令人滿意的成果<br><br>• can't be counted on to deliver on promises<br>無法信賴能否做到答應的事 |

## Communication skills 溝通技巧

| | |
|---|---|
| **Superb**<br>**優秀** | • writes and speaks with remarkable clarity<br>文字和口語表達都非常清楚<br><br>• never gets bogged down in unnecessary details<br>從來不會因為不必要的細節而停滯不前<br><br>• has superior communication skills in person and over the phone<br>具有卓越的面對面和電話溝通技巧<br><br>• develops and delivers imaginative, clear, and concise presentations<br>可做出有創意且清楚扼要的簡報 |

| | |
|---|---|
| **Good**<br>**良好** | • writes and speaks clearly<br>文字和口語表達都很清楚<br>• rarely gets bogged down in unnecessary details<br>很少會因為不必要的細節而停滯不前<br>• has sound communication skills in person and over the phone<br>具有很好的面對面和電話溝通技巧<br>• develops and delivers clear, concise presentations<br>可做出清楚扼要的簡報 |
| **Acceptable**<br>**尚可** | • generally writes and speaks clearly<br>文字和口語表達通常很清楚<br>• usually avoids getting bogged down in unnecessary details<br>通常可避免因不必要的細節而停滯不前<br>• has adequate communication skills in person and over the phone<br>具有不錯的面對面和電話溝通技巧<br>• develops and delivers acceptable presentations<br>可做出令人滿意的簡報 |
| **Needs Improvement**<br>**欠佳** | • sometimes writes and speaks unclearly and with undue complexity<br>文字和口語表達有時不太清楚，內容過於複雜<br>• sometimes gets bogged down in unnecessary details<br>有時會因為不必要的細節而停滯不前 |

| | |
|---|---|
| | • sometimes struggles to communicate in person and over the phone<br>有時很難與人面對面或透過電話溝通<br><br>• develops and delivers presentations in need of further work and polish<br>所做的簡報需要再加強和潤飾 |
| **Poor**<br>**極差** | • writes and speaks unclearly and with undue complexity<br>文字和口語表達不清楚，內容過於複雜<br><br>• gets bogged down in unnecessary details<br>會因為不必要的細節而停滯不前<br><br>• fails to communicate effectively in person and over the phone<br>無法有效的面對面或透過電話溝通<br><br>• develops and delivers presentations that ramble and lack clarity<br>所做的簡報雜亂無章、含糊不清 |

## 重點回顧

- 收集事實數據以預做準備：記下員工這一年來的績效表現，在寫考績表前，先查看紀錄。針對要考核的員工，請其他同仁提供意見回饋，並仔細審閱員工的自評表。
- 使用本章提供的評語範例來協助說明你的評分概念。
- 寫完概括性的評語後，別忘了提供可作為佐證的具體實例。

## • NOTE •

附錄 A

# 寫作四階段的檢查清單

## A Checklist for the Four Stages of Writing

| | |
|---|---|
| **狂人（Madman）** | □ 想想自己為何而寫：你的動機、任務以及想達成的目標為何？<br>□ 想想你的目標讀者是誰，他們需要知道哪些內容。<br>□ 確認自己有多少時間，大致安排從收集構想和資料、擬定大綱、撰寫初稿到修改細節等各階段的時間表。<br>□ 做研究時要運用想像力並充滿熱忱，記下發掘到的相關資訊。<br>□ 敦促自己發揮創意，不要滿足於任何人都想得到的顯而易見的想法。 |
| **建築師（Architect）** | □ 快速以完整句子寫下三個重點，盡可能越具體越好。<br>□ 考量三個重點的最佳順序，必要時可重新排序。 |

| | |
|---|---|
| | ☐ 決定如何安排文件的開頭和結尾。<br>☐ 想想有哪些視覺輔助素材可協助傳達概念。 |
| **木匠（Carpenter）** | ☐ 盡可能遠離所有讓人分心的事物，將手機和電腦通知設為靜音，並空出一小時左右的獨處時間，讓自己專心寫作。<br>☐ 根據所列的三個重點擬定大綱架構。<br>☐ 從你覺得最容易的論點著手，從支持該論點的段落開始寫起，逐一完成每個論點。<br>☐ 盡快的寫，不要停下來編輯或修飾。<br>☐ 盡量一口氣寫完整個段落。如果非得中途起身，先把下一句的頭幾個字寫下後再離開。（再回來後，你會發現比起從頭寫起新的句子，接續已寫一半的句子會容易得多。） |
| **法官（Judge）** | ☐ 完成初稿後，馬上讀過一遍，想想有哪些地方可再加強。<br>☐ 接著，可以的話，休息一個晚上隔天再看；如果時間緊迫，過個幾分鐘再看。<br>☐ 再回頭看初稿時，從目標讀者的角度思考。內容對所有讀者來說是否清楚，是否必須了解內情才能看懂？是否夠簡潔，有沒有贅字浪費讀者的時間？<br>☐ 找出初稿最大的兩個缺失，並試著修正問題。<br>☐ 問問自己：<br>• 有沒有遺漏任何重要資訊？<br>• 是否已強調重點部分？ |

- 每個句子的意思是否清楚、正確？
- 文章轉折是否順暢？
- 在不犧牲重要內容的前提下，可以刪減哪些地方？
- 是否有任何段落太過籠統，可提供具體事證加以補強？
- 是否有任何段落太過沉悶，用字可更活潑生動？
- 遣詞用字是否可再加強？
- 標點符號是否需要改善？
- 有沒有任何錯字？

## • NOTE •

附錄 B

# 不可不知的十二條文法規則

## A Dozen Grammatical Rules You Absolutely Need to Know

### 1. 以And或But作為句子開頭完全不成問題。

想要寫作如行雲流水般順暢，最最重要的元素，就是在句子和段落間有效的運用轉折詞。而效果最卓著的轉折詞，莫過於and和but這兩個最簡單的單音節單字。

長久以來，對於句子以連接詞開頭是不合文法的這個觀念，一流的作家早已不予理會，著名的語法學家也對此提出駁斥。看看各大報的專欄，或瀏覽任何用心編輯的雜誌內頁，你會發現這樣的用法比比皆是。為什麼？因為連接詞其實是絕佳的銜接工具，可清楚點出前後句子的承接關係，更因為這類連接詞簡短、直接、俐落。比起additionally和however這些冗長的連接副詞，不但使音節變多，後面還得多加個逗號，使用and和but通常效果更好。

### 2. 以介系詞作為句子結尾也完全不是問題。

句子不得以介系詞結尾的這個「規則」，是根據拉丁語語法而來的一個極不合理的觀念，有少數（非常少數）十九世紀的作家曾闡述此概念。但長久以來，語法學家已摒棄此觀念，認為這項規定沒有根據也沒有必要。

一般來說，比起刻意避開以介系詞結尾的句子，句尾為介系詞的句子聽起來會更自然得多。試比較以下兩句：What will the new product be used for?（這項新產品有哪些用途？）和 For what purpose will the new product be used?（這項新產品可用於什麼用途？）

不過話說回來，一個句子要有力，通常結尾要夠力，因為句尾是整個句子最能突顯重點的位置。而介系詞鮮少能為句子帶來強而有力的結尾，但這並沒有不合文法。

### 3. 形容詞 good 的副詞是 well。

描述一個人的表現、行為、動作等狀態時，要用副詞 well 來修飾：<The intern works well under pressure>（這位實習生能在壓力下把工作做好）<The research and development stage is going well>（研發階段進行得很順利）<We wish them well in the future>（我們祝福他們未來一切順利）。

雖然有越來越多人把 good 當作副詞來用，但這並非標準英語：<The vice presidents *worked good as a team>（幾位副總裁團隊合作的默契良好）<The new water pump *is running good>（新的水泵運作正常）。

只要被問到 "How are you doing?"（你好嗎？），常常就有人會問到底該用 good 還是 well。在假定正面回覆的情況下，最好的回答是 "I'm doing well"（我很好）（或 "I'm fine, thank you."（我很好，謝謝。）），回答 "I'm good" 雖然常見，但不夠得體。至於回答 "I'm *doing good."則不是標準用法，因為good在這裡是當作副詞用。而某些固定用語則屬於例外情況，可將good作副詞用：<a good many more>（相當多的）<did it but good>（做得非常好）。

### 4. 動詞的單複數取決於句子的主詞。

主詞和動詞的單複數必須一致，例如：Grammar Girl says so（文法女孩這麼說）（Grammar Girl和says皆為單數），All grammarians say so（所有文法學家都這麼說）（Grammarians和say皆為複數）。這個規則看似基本到不值一提，但有很多情況容易出錯。以介系詞片語修飾的主詞就是常見的錯誤來源：an oversupply of foreign imports應該用單數還是複數動詞呢？答案是單數，這樣才能與主詞oversupply一致。至於複合主詞雖然多是用複數動詞，但有時這類主詞其實是表達單數的概念：<The company's bread and butter is still shipping>（這家公司的生計還是以運輸為主）。主詞bread and butter在形式上是複數，但在意義上卻是單數，所以採用單數動詞is。

there（作為虛主詞用時，例如：There is another way）則牽扯出另一個特別的問題，有些專家認為這個問題是現今最常見的文法錯誤。在倒裝句中，真正的主詞在動詞之後：<There go our fourth-quarter profits>（我們的第四季的利潤沒了），主詞profits在動詞go之後。但有些人不管後面接什麼，看到there就是用單數動詞，於是就錯誤百出：<*There is still market capacity and established competition to be considered>（還有市場能力和現有的競爭必須考慮）。複合主詞 capacity and competition應搭配複數動詞are，而不是單數動詞is。

看似複合主詞的情況也常會出問題，比如當句型中有together with和as well as這類用詞時，這些用詞並不構成複數主詞：<The board, along with the president and CFO, endorses the stock split>（董事會和總裁及財務長都贊成股票分割），主詞是單數的board，因此搭配單數動詞endorses。

## 5. 以either和neither作為主詞時，應採用單數動詞。

對於含有複數受詞的介系詞片語所造成的干擾，必須特別留意，主詞either或neither依舊是單數：<Either of the marketing plans involves [而非involve] capital investment>（這兩個行銷計畫中，有其中一個涉及資本投入）<Neither of our expansion options provides [而非provide] a total solution>（這兩個拓展選項都未提供完整的解決方案）。

## 6. 當neither/nor和either/or位於主詞位置時，動詞單複數以第二個主詞元素為準。

當相關連接詞either/or或neither/nor所表達的選項為單數時，動詞即為單數：<Either phone or fax is acceptable for your response>（透過電話或傳真回覆皆可）。當選項為複數時，動詞即為複數：<Neither our accountants nor our lawyers are concerned about the merger>（我們的會計和律師都不擔心併購案）。但是若其中一個選項為單數，另一個為複數，動詞應與第二個選項一致：<Neither the regional managers nor the vice-president for sales likes [而非like] the proposed campaign's theme>（地區經理和銷售副總裁都不喜歡提議的行銷活動主題）<Either the home office or the branch managers

are [而非is] largely responsible for employee morale>（公司總部或分公司經理要為員工士氣負起很大的責任）。

### 7. 無詞尾變化副詞（例如thus或doubtless）不是以-ly結尾。

大部分的副詞是在形容詞字尾加上-ly（large變成largely，quick變成quickly），或是將字尾的-able改成-ably（amicable 變成amicably，capable變成capably）。但英文中也有不少副詞並非以-ly結尾（例如fast、ill和seldom）。對於這類副詞，在字尾加-ly既不必要，也不自然，最常被誤用的兩個例子是*doubtlessly和*thusly。

### 8. however、therefore和otherwise必須加上其他標點符號，才可連接獨立的子句。

獨立的子句必須(1)包含主詞和動詞，以及(2)表達完整的意思；既可單獨成句，也可藉由逗號和連接詞（例如and、but、or）與其他子句連接：<The new advertising campaign is ready, but the CEO has yet to approve it>（新的廣告行銷活動已準備就緒，但執行長尚未批准）。當兩個獨立子句是由連接副詞（例如however）所連接，則連接副詞前須加分號，後面須加逗號：<Mr. Bingham can't attend the meeting; however, he hopes to call before we adjourn>（賓漢先生無法參加會議，但他希望能在我們結束會議之前來電）。若省略分號或以逗號取代，會形成所謂的「逗號拼接句」(comma splice)：<*We were supposed to arrive at 4:00 p.m., however, we didn't arrive until 5:00>（我們應該在下午四點前抵達，但我們直到五點才到）。

## 9. 句中有動詞詞組時，副詞的位置通常在第一個助動詞之後。

長久以來，寫作方面的專家都同意將副詞放在詞組中間，是最有力也最自然的位置：<Industry experts have long agreed on the product's effectiveness>（長久以來，業界專家皆認同此產品的效果），放在其他位置不是顯得生硬：<Industry experts long have agreed on the product's effectiveness>，就是感覺荒謬：<Industry experts have agreed long on the product's effectiveness>。對此觀點持反對意見的人，可能是受到古老迷思的影響，認為分離不定詞不合乎語法（實則不然），因為這也是分離動詞的一種：<We expect the new product line and expanded territory to almost double our sales in the next two years>（我們預期新產品系列和所拓展地區，可讓銷量在未來兩年成長近兩倍）。

當詞組中有一個以上的助動詞，最自然的位置通常是放在第一個助動詞之後（例如has long been assumed）。

## 10. 關係代名詞（that、which和who）必須緊跟在先行詞之後。

關係代名詞（that、which、who、whom，以及字尾加上-ever的變化形）的用途可分為兩種。第一，可連接從屬子句和獨立子句：<Whoever wants to participate is welcome>（任何人想要參加都歡迎），從屬子句(whoever wants to participate)在此是作為主要子句的主詞。第二，可連接子句與先行詞：<Those who want to participate are welcome>（想要參加的人都歡迎）。在此句中，從屬子句(who want to participate)是為先行詞those補充重要資訊。

在第二種句型中，關係代名詞應盡量靠近先行詞，最好是緊跟在先行詞之後。關係代名詞指稱的對象若不清楚，可能會造成困擾，因此必須確保兩者的關聯明確：<*Please discuss the customer-service position in the accounting department that is being eliminated>（請討論要裁撤的會計部門客服職位）。在這句話中，被裁撤的是職位還是部門？我們可將此句改寫以釐清意思：<Please discuss the customer-service position that is being eliminated in the accounting department>（請討論會計部門中要裁撤的客服職位）。改寫後，關係代名詞that便緊跟在先行詞customer-service position之後。

## 11. 同位語提供的若非句子的必要資訊，會以逗號分隔（非限定）；若為必要資訊，則不須以逗號分隔（限定）。

同位語是接在另一個名詞（或代名詞）之後的名詞或名詞片語，用以辨別或補充說明：<My colleague Pat agrees>（我同事派特同意）<The customer, a tall man in an oversized suit, left his keys on the counter>（那位身材高大、穿著寬大外套的顧客把他的鑰匙留在櫃檯上）。

在第一個例句中，同位語Pat並未以逗號與整個句子區隔開來，第二個例句中的a tall man in an oversized suit則用了逗號區隔。之所以有這樣的不同，是因為同位語和關係子句（由which、who 和 whom引導的子句）一樣，對整句的語意來說，可能是必要的，也可能是非必要的。第一個例句中的Pat就屬於必要資訊，用以指明所說的是哪一位同事（可能有很多位同事）。而在第二個例句，同位語則只是補充說明額外資訊。我們也可以說第一個例句中的Pat限定了colleague所指稱的對象，第二句的同位語則為非限定用法。時下的寫作書多是用「限定」和「非限定」來稱呼這些同位語。

除了逗號外，同位語也可以用長破折號（通常是用於強調）或括號（通常是為了弱化其重要性）來做區隔。

## 12. 相關連接詞（成對的連接詞）的結構須平行對稱。

相關連接詞（例如both... and、neither... nor和not only... but also）皆為成對出現，用以連接語法一致的相關結構，且連接詞所修飾的詞類應緊接在每個連接詞後。單純連接名詞時，使用平行結構不太會有問題：<neither time nor money>，但連接片語或子句時，就有點麻煩，例如以下這句錯誤示範：*We not only raised our regional market share but also our profit margin（我們不僅提高了地區市占率，也提高了淨利率），這句應改寫成：We raised not only our regional market share but also our profit margin。動詞raised必須放在第一個相關連接詞(not only)之外，使兩個連接的結構皆為所有格片語（our regional market share 和 our profit margin）。

附錄C

# 不可不知的十二條標點符號規則

## A Dozen Punctuation Rules You Absolutely Need to Know

### 1. 形容詞短語應以連字號連接。

small-business incentive（小型企業的誘因）和small business incentive（微小的商業誘因）兩者的意思不同；limited-liability clause（有限責任條款）和limited liability clause（有限制的責任條款）的意思也不同。當兩個以上的單字合成一個字來修飾名詞，中間必須以連字號連接（在某些情況下除外）。因此，飯店客房門口告知服務人員請勿打擾的牌子叫作"do-not-disturb sign"，開業二十五年的公司是一家"25-year-old company"。

但也有部分例外情況：(1)以-ly副詞和當作形容詞的過去分詞合組成的簡單短語不加連字號：<a greatly exaggerated claim>（極度誇大的宣稱）。(2)以專有名詞組成的短語：<New Zealand exports>（紐西蘭的出口商品）或外來字組成的短語：<a post facto rationalization>（事後合理化）不加連字號。(3)一般來說，放在修飾的名詞之後的形容詞短語不加連字號：<a job well done>（做得很好的工作），但也有因使用習慣而例外的情況：<our HR manager

is risk-averse by nature>（我們的人事經理生性不愛冒險）<the information is time-sensitive>（這項資訊具有時效性）。

### 2. 列舉三個以上的項目時，and或or之前須加上逗號。

雖然在簡單的序列中<red, white, and blue>，在連接詞前可能不需要加所謂的「系列逗號」(serial comma)，意思也很清楚，但序列若變得較長、較複雜，語意清晰度也會隨之驟降：<We hope to boost sales in the target area, to build the company's name recognition statewide and beyond, and to attract investors for possible franchise opportunities.>（我們希望提高目標區域的銷量，在國內外打響公司知名度，以及吸引投資者以尋求可能的加盟機會。）。所以，到底應遵循什麼規則？

《The Chicago Manual of Style》和其他關於專業、技術和學術寫作的權威，幾乎一致贊成只要是列舉項目，都應使用系列逗號，贊成的原因很充分：不加逗號有時可能會出錯（導致語意不清或其他更糟的情況），加上逗號則絕對不會錯。

### 3. 句子中有兩個複合謂語時，無須以逗號分隔；但若有三個以上的複合謂語，則須用標點符號加以分隔。一般多使用逗號，但若為了釐清語意，必要時也可用分號。

當兩個謂語的主詞相同時，我們通常不會重複主詞。如果第二個子句重複了主詞，則應在連接詞之前加上逗號：<I stopped by yesterday, and I will call today>（我昨天順道造訪，今天會致電聯絡）。但若未重複主詞（即兩個謂語共用主詞），連接詞之前則無須加上逗號：<I stopped by yesterday and will call today>。當合併三個以上像這樣的子句（即共用相同主詞），這些謂語便形成了序列，且至少必須以一個逗號加以分隔：<I wrote him yesterday, stopped by yesterday, and will call today>（我昨天寫信給他並順道造訪，今天會致電聯絡）。

若在這些序列中，有部分謂語已包含逗號，則應改用分號來加以分隔：<I wrote him last week; I stopped by yesterday with the paperwork, the deposit check, and the keys; and I will call him today>（我上週寫信給他，昨天帶了文件、存款支票和鑰匙順道造訪，今天會致電聯絡。）。相同的原則也適用於複合謂語：<I wrote him last week; stopped by yesterday with the paperwork, the deposit check, and the keys; and will call him today>。

### 4. 形成複數名詞時，不要加上撇號。

在形成複數名詞時（而非所有格或縮讀字），若加上撇號，大多時候幾乎都是錯誤的用法。大多數專有名詞只需要加-s，以-s、-x、-z和嘶音-ch或-sh結尾的名詞則是加-es。不須加撇號的例外情況是遇到小寫字母：<Mind your p's and q's>（注意你的言行舉止，p's和q's分別為pleases和thank-yous的縮寫），和大寫字母：<all A's on the audit report>（審計報告中所有項目都得到A），此時加上撇號可防止產生誤解。至於數字或沒有縮寫點的大寫縮寫字，若要形成複數，則不須加撇號：<ATMs became ubiquitous in the 1990s>（自助提款機在 1990 年代變得普遍存在）。一般的單字和字母若要形成複數形，通常是將該單字或字母改成斜體，再以標準字體加上-s：<Please delete the first two *or*s in the sentence>（請將這句的前兩個or刪掉）。

形成姓名的複數形時，特別常看到誤加撇號的情況。史密斯先生和史密斯太太是the Smiths，不是*the Smith's（也不是*the Smiths'）；史蒂文斯先生和史蒂文斯太太則是the Stevenses（而不是*the Steven's或*the Stevens'）。

### 5. 除非主詞和動詞之間有修飾的插入語存在，否則不要將文法上的主詞和動詞分開。

一般來說，互相搭配的字詞就應該緊接在一起，盡量不要分得太開。所以像同位語就會跟在修飾的名詞或代名詞之後：<Maeve Peterson, the new CEO, is...>（新任執行長梅夫彼得森⋯），代名詞也不該離所指稱的先行詞太遠，以免之間的連結不夠清楚。基於相同的原則，句子的主詞和動詞最好也靠近在一起，以免句子東拉西扯，偏離了主題。

但這並不是說在主詞和動詞間插入短語或子句一定是錯的，在修飾語意或補充資訊方面，插入語可發揮很好的效果：<Ms. Peterson, whose leadership at McLaughlin Enterprises has been credited with that firm's turnaround, will take the reins here on June 1.>（彼得森女士的領導能力，從麥克勞克林企業這家公司的徹底轉型即可見一斑，而她將於6月1日接掌本公司。）。雖然這種句法可以更強調修飾語的部分，但若把插入的短語或子句放在開頭，讓主詞和動詞更靠近，通常可讓語意更加清楚：<Credited with turning around McLaughlin Enterprises during her four years as CEO, Ms. Peterson starts work here on June 1>（彼得森女士在擔任麥克勞克林企業執行長的四年間，成功徹底改造了這家公司，而她將於6月1日開始在本公司工作）。

## 6. 使用項目符號吸引目標讀者注意，但不要過度使用。

項目符號可吸引讀者目光注意條列式重點，且不限定順序。理想的條列方式皆遵循以下規則：

- 在列點之前，以一句說明作為引言，並在句尾加上冒號。
- 將所有條列項目採用相同的文法結構（例如全為名詞片語，或全為以動詞開頭的謂語），長度也應盡可能相近。
- 以首行凸排的格式來條列項目。如此一來，項目符號便會突出於左側，所有同類的項目符號也都會對齊。
- 所有條列項目應採單行間距，但在每個項目之間，可額外多留一點空間。
- 項目符號應採用簡單的樣式，避免奇形怪狀或藝術風格的符號，建議使用實心圓點，尺寸約為小寫字母o的大小。

和其他任何為了突顯重點或吸引讀者注意力的設計一樣，若過度使用，會使條列要點的效果大打折扣。

## 7. 避免用引號來強調字詞。

引號可用來表達多種不同涵義，其中以標示引語這個固有的用法最為常見。有時，引號也隱含諷刺的態度<an “expert” in negotiation>（談判「專家」），或可能暗示引號中的內容根本不是字面上的意思<Here’s the “final” schedule>（這份是「最終」時程表。）。引號也可用來引介詞語，和我們說「所謂的…」涵義相同。鑒於引號有上述這些可能的不同解釋，用引號來強調字詞並不是一個很好的選擇。傳統上，採用斜體字更能毫無歧義的表達強調的意思。

此外，也應避免：(1)使用底線，在打字機的年代，底線具有和斜體字一樣的功用，但不如斜體字美觀；(2)過度使用粗體字，最好將粗體保留給名稱和標題使用；以及(3)全為大寫字母，全大寫的字若超過一到兩個，會令人感到厭煩，且難以閱讀。

### 8. 大多數帶有字首的字不需要加連字號。

美式英語通常不喜歡在字首和字根之間加上連字號（例如：anteroom、biennial、deselect、proactive、quarterfinal、semisweet），即使會因此重複相同字母，也不須插入連字號（cooperate、reelect、misspeak）。但也有幾個例外情況：(1)為了避免產生誤解或歧義（re-create、re-lease、re-sign）；(2)當字根為專有名詞時(pre-Halloween sales)；以及(3)使用特定字首時，例如all-(all-inclusive)、ex-(ex-partner)和self-(self-correcting)。

### 9. 在稱呼語之後，使用冒號或逗號，不要用分號。

在商業信件往來中，使用冒號是標準用法：<Dear Ms. Wilson:>；若為私人信件，則可使用逗號：<Dear Barbara,>。在商業信件中，視寄件者和收件者的私人關係而定，可能也可用逗號，但使用分號絕對是錯誤用法：(*Dear Mr. Jones;)。

### 10. 長破折號有兩個合理且極具價值的功用：用於分隔和強調。

首先，長破折號—即所謂em-dash—可框住本質上為附帶說明的內容，使內容更為突顯。注意看第一句中的「即所謂em-dash」是如何達到更顯眼的效果。若要將這幾個字與句子的其他部分區隔，大可以用逗號或括號，但用破折號更可特別強調插入語的部分（用括號則像是在拜託目標讀者略過不看）。善用長破折號是個很有力的寫作技巧，但和所有效果卓著的寫作技巧一樣，不宜過度使用。

其次，長破折號可用來插入簡短的附註，並與句子的主要部分隔開，相當於取代冒號的功用，但多了幾分強調的效果。隔開的部分可以在句首：<Customer service—it's our top priority>（顧客服務是我們的首要之務），也可在句尾：<No matter what the field, an able workforce starts with and continues with one thing—professional training>（無論是在哪個領域，要培養有能力的員工並持續精進，都得仰賴專業訓練）。

## 11. 寫月分和年分時不需要加逗號。

長久以來，格式指南皆同意在月分和年分間不應該加逗號：<February 2012>。依美國標準格式「月／日／年」寫日期時，必須在日期後加上逗號：<February 23, 2012>；採用「日／月／年」格式時，則無需逗號：<23 February 2012>。在年分之後也須加逗號：<Groundbreaking was held February 23,2012, in Menomonee Falls.>（破土儀式已於2012年2月23日在梅諾莫尼瀑布舉辦。），但將日期作為形容詞用時除外：<the February 23, 2012 groundbreaking ceremonies>（2012年2月23日的破土儀式）。

## 12. 形成單數名詞的所有格時，一律加上's，即使字尾是-s、-z、-x或-ss亦然。

在史壯克與懷特合著的經典書籍《英文寫作風格的要素》(The Elements of Style)一書中，第一條規則即為：單數名詞的所有格是在字尾加's：<Kansas's business climate>（堪薩斯州的商業環境）

<Holtz's contract>（霍爾茲的合約）<Xerox's patents>（全錄公司的專利）<the actress's endorsement>（女演員的代言）。但請注意，人稱代名詞和who有自己的所有格形式，無須加上's（mine、our、ours、your、yours、his、her、hers、its、their、theirs、whose）。此外，如果公司或其他實體的名稱是由複數名詞組成，則只須加上撇號：<United Airlines' quarterly report>（聯合航空公司的季度報告）<The United Arab Emirates' capital is Abu Dhabi>（阿拉伯聯合大公國的首都是阿布達比）。

若要形成複數名詞的所有格，請在該字詞的標準複數形式字尾的-s後加上撇號：<caterers' fees>（外燴業者的費用）<the bosses' offices>（老闆的辦公室）。非以-s結尾的複數名詞則為例外，這類名詞應遵循與單數名詞所有格相同的規則：<a line of children's clothing>（童裝系列）<the alumnae's reunion>（女校友的聚會）。

附錄 D

# 常見錯誤用法

## Common Usage Gaffes

以下列出二十個常見的錯誤用法，寫得馬虎和寫得用心的分別，一看便知。錯誤的字詞前皆以星號加以標示。

| ✕ 錯誤示範： | ○ 正確示範： |
|---|---|
| I *feel badly about the oversight. | I feel bad about the oversight.<br>對於此疏忽，我感到很抱歉。 |
| I'm *feeling very well about the sales figures.<br>我對銷售數字感到很滿意。 | I feel good (contented).<br>I feel well (healthy).<br>我覺得很好（滿足）。<br>我覺得很好（健康）。 |
| They're *doing good. | They're doing well.<br>他們過得還不錯。 |
| Just *between you and I. | Just between you and me.<br>這是我們之間的祕密。 |

| | |
|---|---|
| He expected *Helen and I to help him. | He expected Helen and me to help him.<br>他期望海倫和我會幫他。 |
| She *could care less. | She couldn't care less.<br>她一點也不在乎。 |
| He's *laying down on the couch. | He's lying down on the couch.<br>他躺在沙發上。 |
| *Where are you at? | Where are you?<br>你在哪裡？ |
| *If I would have been there... | If I had been there...<br>如果我在那裡⋯ |
| She serves on the board; *as such, she has fiduciary duties. | She's a board member; as such, she has fiduciary duties.<br>她是董事會成員，因此負有信託責任。 |
| The letter was sent *on accident. | The letter was sent by accident.<br>這封信是不小心寄出的。 |
| I *wish he was faster. | I wish he were faster.<br>我希望他能更快一點。 |
| I *could of done it. | I could have done it.<br>我本來可以做的。 |
| *in regards to | in regard to, or regarding<br>關於 |

| ✕ 錯誤示範： | ○ 正確示範： |
|---|---|
| *less items | fewer items<br>更少項目 |
| He was *undoubtably guilty. | He was undoubtedly guilty.<br>他無疑是有罪的。 |
| *preventative | preventive<br>預防的 |
| *There's lots of reasons. | There are lots of reasons.<br>有很多原因。 |
| *as best as she can | as best she can<br>盡力 |
| *irregardless | regardless, or irrespective<br>無論 |

若要了解更多正確用法，請參閱附錄F。

## • NOTE •

附錄 E

# 商業寫作禮儀注意事項

## Some Dos and Don'ts of Business Writing Etiquette

**建議事項：**

1. 送出任何文件之前，務必要檢查校對，以確保拼字和文法正確。
2. 再次確認收件人的名字拼寫是否正確，頭銜是否適當（Ms.、Mrs.、Miss、Mr.、Dr.、Judge、Justice、Honorable等）。如果有信封，別忘了也要檢查信封。
3. 除非你與收件人是朋友，否則商業信件署名時，應簽署全名。若使用的稱呼語是"Dear Mr. Smith,"，請簽署全名；如果是"Dear George,"，則可只簽名字。
4. 以墨水筆簽署信件，不要使用簽名印章。
5. 一律附上你的聯絡資訊，以確保收件人知道回覆時如何與你聯絡。
6. 若要寄送手寫信件給商業聯絡人或朋友，請使用郵票來郵寄信件，不要用郵資機在信封上蓋郵資。
7. 寄出電子郵件之前，請務必檢查：(a)已在收件人欄位加入所有收件人地址，以及(b)已附上你在信中提到的所有附件。
8. 有效利用留白空間，以確保文件版面易讀，不會使目標讀者看得吃力。保持寬敞的邊界，在段落間保留間距，視需要以副標題加以分段，並可適當的縮排。

9. 註明文件撰寫日期（電子郵件除外，因為郵件本身即附有日期），讓讀者有可參照的時間。

10. 若要寫感謝函給同在一個辦公室的多位同事，應分別撰寫不同內容。如果大量複製相同內容，被收件人比較發現後，反而會產生反效果。

**避免事項：**

1. 不要使用全大寫，全部大寫的文字像是在向目標讀者大聲喊叫。
2. 回信給寄件人時，不要為了省時間或省紙，而寫在原始的信件上。回信時，即使只是簡短的一封信，也應寫在另外一張紙上。至於合約和其他協議則另當別論。
3. 不要說"Thank you in advance"。若要在提出要求時向人致謝，直接說出請求，然後說"Thank you"即可。此外，當事情完成後，也別忘了再次道謝（或也可當面致謝）。
4. 除非確定真有必要，否則寄送電子郵件時，不要使用密件副本。使用密件副本可能會讓人認為你欠缺考慮。
5. 不要使用過小或太特殊的字型，以免造成閱讀上的困難，或讓自己顯得輕佻。
6. 電子郵件主旨行的標題不宜過長。
7. 寫感謝函時，不要寫在印有"Thank you!"或Merci等字樣的卡片上（這麼做會讓人覺得失禮）。
8. 若直覺告訴你應該要寫信表達恭喜、感謝、慰問或其他任何心情，不要因為時間的流逝而裹足不前。

9. 不要在憤怒或沮喪的情緒下寫信。退一步，沉澱一下，將自己從目前的情況抽離。等你有時間認真思考，能冷靜的表達意見後，再回去寫信。
10. 如果所寫的東西被報導在媒體上公諸於世，會讓你感到羞愧難堪，就表示不該寫那樣的內容。

## · NOTE ·

附錄 F

# 正確用字入門

## A Primer of Good Usage

**abstruse** 請見obtuse。

**accede; exceed** accede = 同意或應允 <We acceded to your request>（我們同意你的要求）。exceed = 超過、超出 <Your needs exceeded our capacity for production>（你的需求超過我們的生產能力）。

**access; excess** 傳統上，兩者皆為名詞。access = 接近或進入的行為或機會。excess = 超過所需要的數量。當然，access現在也常作為動詞，意為「存取；滲入」<I couldn't access those files>（我無法存取那些檔案）<I accessed the storage unit>（我進入了儲藏室）。

**accord; accordance** accord = 協議 <The partners are in accord about expanding plant capacity>（合作夥伴對擴充產能意見一致）。accordance = 符合 <The materials weren't in accordance with our specs>（材料不符合我們的規格）。

**administer; administrate** 前者為標準用法，administer = 掌管、施

行。*administrate則是由administration反向構詞衍生而來，應避免使用。

**admission; admittance** admission = 進入的許可或權利<The price of admission is steep>（門票價格高昂）。admittance =「實際進入」的行為<No admittance after 6 p.m.>（晚上六點後不許進入）。

**adopt; adapt** adopt = 採納以作為己用<Adopt this cause>（採納這個原因）。adapt = 調整<Adapt your leadership style>（調整你的領導風格）。請注意，它們的名詞分別為adoption和adaptation。

**adverse; averse** adverse = 不利的或相反的<The expansion plan was postponed in face of adverse market conditions>（由於不利的市場條件，已暫緩擴充計畫）。averse = 反對或不願意的；嫌惡、恐懼或有敵意的<The company is risk-averse>（這家公司傾向迴避風險）。

**advise; advice** advise是動詞<Our CFO advised against the merger>（財務長反對併購），advice則是名詞<We took the consultant's advice>（我們採納了顧問的建議）。

**affect; effect** affect一般作動詞用，意為「影響」<The ordinance may affect our sales>（這條法令可能會影響我們的銷售）。effect則多作為名詞，意指結果或效果<It may be a positive effect>（可能會是正面的效果），但effect也可當作動詞，意為「實行」<The new manager effected several changes>（新來的經理實行了幾項變更）。

**aggravate; irritate** aggravate = 使惡化<This news aggravates an already-bad situation>（這個新聞使本就糟糕的局面更加惡化）。irritate = 使

惱怒。口語上常會用aggravate來表示irritate的意思，但仍有些人不喜歡這種用法。

**aide; aid** aide是助手，aid是協助。

**allusion; illusion** allusion = 對某個文化作品、歷史事件或其他大家所熟知事物的暗指<"Sage of Omaha" is an allusion to Warren Buffett>（巴菲特被譽為「奧瑪哈的聖人」）。illusion = 錯覺或假象<Their profitability turned out to be an illusion>（結果他們的獲利能力其實只是假象）。

**a lot** 一律為分開的兩個字。

**already; all ready** already = 之前，已經<She was already taking notes>。（她原本就已在做筆記了）all ready = 完全準備就緒<The corporate minutes were all ready for the secretary's sign-off>（公司會議紀錄已全部準備好，就等祕書簽名）。

**alternative; alternate** 作為名詞，alternative = 兩個或多個選擇中的一個選擇<We came up with an alternative design>（我們想出了另一款設計）；alternate = 代替者<The delegate's alternate attended>（會議由代表的代理人出席）。

**altogether; all together** altogether = 全部或完全<This trip was altogether useless>（這趟旅程毫無用處）。all together = 共同或全體<That day we reported to him all together>（那天我們全體向他報告）。

**ambiguous; ambivalent** ambiguous = 模稜兩可的<Please clarify the ambiguous policy>（請釐清這條模稜兩可的政策）。ambivalent = 心情

矛盾的<The CFO has ambivalent feelings about the trade-off>（財務長對這個權衡取捨感到矛盾）。

**amend; emend** amend = 增修文件，尤指法律或其他法務文件<Amend the contract>（修訂合約內容）。emend = 校訂或修改文稿<Emend the proposal before you circulate it>（將提案發給大家之前，先進行校對）。

**among** 請見between。

**amuse; bemuse** amuse = 娛樂或使開心。bemuse = 使困惑。

**antidote; anecdote** antidote = 應對難題的解決方法<Preparation is the antidote for nervousness>（做好準備是克服緊張的解方）。anecdote = 具說明性質的趣聞軼事<She told an anecdote about her first day on the job>（她說了關於第一天上班的趣事）。

**anxious; eager** anxious = 預期中帶著焦慮不安的情緒<We grew anxious about the IPO>（我們對於首次公開募股越來越焦慮）。eager = 預期中帶著熱切的心情<Customers were eager for the retail stores to open>（顧客們熱切期待零售店的開幕）。

**appraise; apprise** appraise = 估價<Appraise the property at $1 million>（此資產的估價為一百萬美金）。apprise = 通知<Apprise me of any changes>（如有任何變化，請通知我）。

**arbiter; arbitrator** arbiter = 具有最終決定權的裁決者<You're the arbiter of company policy>（你是公司政策的裁決者）。arbitrator = 主持仲裁以解決爭議的仲裁人<The arbitrator decided the dispute in our

favor>（仲裁人對此爭議的判決對我們有利）。

**as** 請見like。

**assure; ensure; insure** assure = 做出保證以使對方放心 <He assured me he'd attend>（他向我保證他會出席）。ensure = 確保某事會發生或如預期進行 <We made a schedule to ensure that we'd meet our deadline>（我們排定時程以確保如期完成）。insure = 投保以免於損失或損害 <The warehouse was insured for less than market value>（倉庫的投保金額低於市值）。

**attain; obtain** attain = 達成或完成某事 <The regional division attained its quarterly sales target>（地區分店達成了每季銷售目標）。obtain = 獲得某物 <We had no trouble obtaining raw materials>（我們輕鬆的取得了原料）。

**averse** 請見adverse。

**avocation** 請見vocation。

**awhile; a while** awhile為副詞，表示「一會兒」<Let's talk awhile before deciding>（我們先討論一下再決定）。a while則是名詞片語，意為「一段時間」<Let's talk for a while before deciding>（我們先討論一下再決定）。

**bear; born; borne** bear = (1)帶有或負載 <Corporate suitors come bearing gifts>（有意收購者帶著有利條件而來），或(2)生育 <bear a child>（生孩子）。borne自語意1衍生而來 <Airborne particulates make the product unsafe>（空中的微粒對產品造成安全疑慮），born則衍生

自語意2<You're a born leader>（你是天生的領導者）。

**bemuse** 請見amuse。

**beside; besides** beside = (1)在旁邊或在一側<The seat beside the window is taken>（靠窗的座位已經有人了），或(2)超出<That's beside the point>（這已經離題了）<she was beside herself with joy>（她非常的快樂）。besides = 除了…之外<Besides coffee, we sell tea and baked goods>（除了咖啡，我們也賣茶和烘焙食品）。

**between; among** between著重於一對一的關係<Between payroll and health care, our costs are up>（我們在工資和健康保險方面的成本增加了），即使涉及的對象在兩個以上<Talks began between the firm and its various suitors>（公司和不同的有意收購者已展開對談）。among則指在三個以上的對象之間，較為鬆散的關聯<There was one standout among applicants>（應徵者中有一位較為突出）。

**blatant; flagrant** blatant = 公然、明顯的<That's a blatant lie>（這是很明顯的謊言）。flagrant = 明目張膽的無視禮貌和規範<Refusing to shake hands was a flagrant break of protocol>（拒絕握手顯然違反了禮儀規範）。

**bombastic** = 浮誇、誇大的<Bombastic speeches stretched out the meeting>（浮誇的演講延長了會議時間）。這個字與暴力無關。

**born; borne** 請見bear。

**breach; broach** breach = 違反<That's a breach of contract>（這是違反合約的行為），或破壞<Expansion plans will breach the market's

boundaries>（拓展計畫將會違反市場的界限）。broach = 提及 <I hate to broach the subject>（我實在不想提起這個話題）。

**can; may** 最適當的用法是以can表達權力或能力 <We can ship your order next week>（我們可在下週將你訂購的商品出貨），may則用以表達允許或可能 <May we ship your order by UPS?>（我們可透過UPS運送你訂購的商品嗎？）。

**canvas; canvass** canvas = 帆布 <We ordered a canvas awning>（我們訂購了帆布遮雨棚）。canvass = 當名詞時，意為「民調或調查」；若當動詞，意為「進行民調或調查」<Canvass your customers before you brainstorm new products>（發想新產品前，先向顧客展開調查）。

**capital; Capitol** Capitol = 美國國會或州議會開會時所在的國會大廈或州議會大廈。除此以外的其他意思，皆應拼寫為capita l<capital expenses>（資本支出）<capital letter>（大寫字母）<a capital crime>（死罪）<the capital city>（首都）。

**censor; censure** censor = 進行檢查，若判斷內容引人反感，則可能限制發行。censure = 譴責某人。

**clench; clinch** clench = 握緊，尤其用以表示憤怒或決心 <clenched fist>（握緊的拳頭）。clinch = 取得或固定 <clinch the sale>（達成銷售）。

**climatic; climactic** climatic = 與天氣相關，尤其指氣候 <climatic change>（氣候變遷）。climactic = 戲劇性、引人入勝、高潮迭起的 <climactic tension>（戲劇化的張力）。

**clinch** 請見clench。

**closure; cloture** closure = 結束或解決某事的行為或事實。cloture = 終止辯論提付表決的議會程序。

**collaborate; corroborate** collaborate = 在事業上一同合作<We once collaborated in a joint venture>（我們曾合作經營合資公司）。corroborate = 給予支援，尤其指證實資訊<Two studies corroborate the claims>（有兩項研究證實這些主張）。

**common** 請見mutual。

**compare to; compare with** compare A to B是將A比喻為B，著眼於兩者的相似處；compare A with B則是將A與B互相比較，同時著重於相似與相異之處。

**compel; impel** compel = 強迫，尤指藉由權威或出於必要<I felt compelled to report the error>（我覺得必須要舉報錯誤）。impel = 受情況或有力的論證所驅使<Better opportunities impelled her to relocate>（更好的機會驅使她選擇轉調）。

**compendious; voluminous** compendious = 簡潔扼要的。voluminous = 寬鬆、寬敞的。

**complementary; complimentary** complementary = (1)補足或互補的，或(2)相配或和諧的<a bundle of complementary products>（一組互相搭配的產品）。complimentary = (1)免費的<complimentary tickets>（免費門票），或(2)稱讚的<complimentary reviews>（讚美的評論）。

**comprise; compose** comprise = 包含<The company comprises three business units>（這家公司包含三個業務單位）。compose = 組成<The company is composed of three business units>（這家公司由三個業務單位組成）。*is comprised of絕對是錯誤的用法。

**compulsive; compulsory** compulsive = 容易受無法控制的衝動所影響，或是由這些衝動所引起<compulsive behavior>（衝動的行為）。compulsory = 強制的 <compulsory training>（必要的訓練）。

**connote** 請見denote。

**consequent; subsequent** consequent = 作為結果（後果）隨後發生的<Our supplier took responsibility for consequent costs>（我們的供應商負責承擔後續成本）。subsequent = 時間上隨後發生的<Subsequent ads included a disclaimer>（之後的廣告中已包含免責聲明）。

**continual; continuous** continual = 間歇性反覆發生的<continual calls for tech support>（再三致電尋求技術支援）。continuous = 連續不斷的<continuous efforts to meet our goals>（不斷努力以達成目標）。

**convince; persuade** convince... of = 說服，證明論點<convince the board of the need to expand>（說服董事會必須拓展業務）。persuade... to = 說服並使對方採取行動<persuade the board to fund the building program>（說服董事會對建築計畫挹注資金）。

**corroborate** 請見collaborate。

**council; counsel** council = 委員會 <the city council>（市議會）。counsel = (1)顧問 <corporate counsel>（公司法律顧問），(2)忠告<She heeded

the counsel of her CFO>（她聽從財務長的忠告），或(3)提出忠告<My mentor counseled patience>（老師建議我要有耐心）。

**credible; credulous; incredulous; creditable** credible = 可信、可靠的<a credible argument>（可靠的論點）。credulous = 易受騙的<credulous acceptance>（容易輕信的態度）。incredulous = 不相信的<an incredulous audience>（抱持懷疑的觀眾）。creditable = 值得尊敬但非最突出的<a creditable performance>（不錯的表現）。

**damage; damages** damage = 傷害<damage caused by the false rumor>（因為虛假傳言所造成的傷害）。damages = 司法判賠的損害賠償金<judgment for $2 million in damages>（判決兩百萬元賠償金）。

**declaim** 請見disclaim。

**definite; definitive** definite = 清楚、明確、確定的<a definite asset to the department>（該部門的明確資產）。definitive = 可靠的<the definitive source of information>（可靠的資訊來源）。

**delegate** 請見relegate。

**deliberate; deliberative** deliberate = 故意的<a deliberate affront>（蓄意侮辱）。deliberative = 經過討論或商議的<a deliberative decision-making process>（審慎的的決策過程）。

**denote; connote** denote = 表示；指稱<Mortgagee denotes the lender, not the borrower>（抵押權人是指放款人，而非借款人）。connote = 暗示；隱含言外之意<An open workspace connotes collaboration>（開放的工作空間令人聯想到合作）。

**depreciate; deprecate** depreciate = 貶值 <The car will depreciate by 40% when you drive it away>（車子一開上路，馬上就貶值40%）。deprecate = 反對，不贊成 <The manager deprecated the use of company meal allowances for those working solo>（經理反對讓單獨工作的員工使用公司的餐費津貼）。

**detract; distract** detract = 有損於（某種特質）<His abrupt manner detracted from his effectiveness>（他魯莽的態度影響了他的工作成效）。distract = 使分心 <An accomplice distracted the cashier>（一名共犯分散了收銀員的注意力）。

**device; devise** device = 工具或裝置 <a handy device>（方便的裝置）。devise = 創造或發明 <devise a better system>（發明更好的系統）。

**different** 建議使用different from，而不是different than。

**differ from; differ with** differ from的意思為「不同於」<Gross profits differ from net profits>（毛利與淨利不同）；differ with則是指持不同意見 <I differ with you on that point>（關於這點，我和你的看法不同）。

**disburse** 請見disperse。

**disclaim; declaim** disclaim = 否認或拒絕接受 <disclaim any knowledge of the report>（聲明對報告毫不知情）。declaim = 激昂陳述 <declaim against corruption>（嚴詞反對貪腐）。

**discrete; discreet** discrete = 分別的 <three discrete sources of funding>（三個不同的資金來源）。discreet = 謹慎、圓滑的 <a discreet phone

call>（一通謹慎的通話）。

**disinterested; uninterested** disinterested = 公正的；與爭議事項沒有任何利害關係的 <The arbitrator must be a disinterested third party>（仲裁人必須是公正的第三方）。uninterested = 不感興趣的 <The audience was uninterested>（觀眾並不感興趣）。

**disperse; disburse** disperse = 驅散 <disperse an unruly crowd>（驅散混亂的群眾）。disburse = 撥款 <disburse grants>（發放補助金）。

**distinct; distinctive** distinct = 清楚明確的 <We set three distinct goals this quarter>（本季我們設定了三個不同目標）。distinctive = 與眾不同、別具特色的 <her distinctive management style is unlike any we've ever seen>（她獨特的管理風格與我們以往看過的都不同）。

**distract** 請見 detract。

**dominant; dominate** dominant = 占優勢的 <the dominant player>（領先的選手）。dominate = 控制 <dominate the market>（主導市場）。

**eager** 請見 anxious。

**effect** 請見 affect。

**e.g.; i.e.** e.g. = 例如 <big-ticket items (e.g., cars, refrigerators, and furnaces)>（昂貴的物品，例如汽車、冰箱和暖氣爐）。I.e. = 亦即 <numismatics (i.e., coin-collecting)>（錢幣收藏，也就是收集錢幣）。

**elicit; illicit** elicit = 引發反應 <The verbal gaffe elicited laughter>（口誤失言引發哄堂大笑）。illicit = 違禁、非法的 <illicit behavior>（非法

行為）。

**eligible; illegible** eligible = 合格的；合適的。illegible = 因為字跡或印刷等問題而難以辨認的。

**embarrass** 請依此拼法拼寫。

**emend** 請見amend。

**eminent** 請見imminent。

**empathy; sympathy** empathy = 同理心<empathy for a kindred spirit>（對志趣相投者的同理心）。sympathy = 同情心<sympathy for the displaced survivors>（對流離失所的生還者感到同情）。

**ensure** 請見assure。

**equally** 應避免使用*equally as。正確的用法應為equally profitable，而非*equally as profitable。

**evoke; invoke** evoke = 喚起<evoke memories>（喚起記憶）。invoke = 請求，尤指請求獲得權力或協助<invoke the right to counsel>（請求聘請律師的權利）。

**explicit; implicit** explicit = (1)明確的<an explicit disclaimer>（明確的免責聲明），或(2)露骨、駭人的<explicit photos>（露骨的相片）。implicit = (1)不言明的<an implicit warranty>（默示擔保），或(2)絕對的<implicit trust>（絕對的信任）。

**farther; further** farther = 距離上較遠<Drive three miles farther>（再開三英里）。further = 更進一步<Further study is needed>（進修學習

是必要的）。

**faze; phase** faze = 使困擾<not fazed by the rude caller>（不因無理的來電者而困擾）。phase = 事情發展的階段<a growing phase>（成長階段）。

**fewer** 請見less。

**first、second、third** 請依此寫法拼寫，不建議用*firstly、*secondly、*thirdly。

**flagrant** 請見blatant。

**flair; flare** flair = (1)天賦<a flair for pitching ideas>（推銷構想的天分），或(2)獨特風格<write with flair>（展現寫作風格）。flare = 亮光或活動的短暫爆發<an emotional flare-up>（情緒爆發）。

**flaunt; flout** flaunt = 炫耀某物<flaunting new jewelry>（炫耀新的珠寶）。flout = 公然違背或藐視<flouting the rules>（公然違反規則）。

**flounder; founder** flounder = 艱苦掙扎<The campaign was floundering>（活動進行得不順利）。founder = (1)沉沒<The stock foundered when profits fell>（當利潤下降，股價也隨之下跌），(2)失敗<The company foundered after the scandal>（公司在發生醜聞後陷入了困境）。

**forbear; forebear** forbear = 克制衝動<We must forbear any thoughts of retaliating>（我們必須克制任何報復的念頭）。forebear = 祖先<My grandmother and other forebears were mostly Irish>（我的祖母和其他祖先大多是愛爾蘭人）。

**forgo; forego** forgo = 棄絕 <forgo help>（放棄求助）。forego = 在先 <the foregoing events>（之前的事件）。

**formally; formerly** formally= 正式的 <We haven't been formally introduced>（我們還沒正式的互相介紹）。formerly= 以前 <He was formerly with Hastings>（他之前在黑斯廷公司工作）。

**founder** 請見flounder。

**further** 請見farther。

**gibe; jibe** gibe = 嘲弄或嘲笑 <The manager's talk was interrupted by good-natured gibes>（經理的談話被不帶惡意的嘲諷給打斷）。jibe = 相符 <That jibes with what I expected>（這和我的預期相符）。

**harass** 請依此拼法拼寫。

**horde; hoard** horde = 一大群人 <hordes of customers>（一大群顧客）。hoard = 貯藏，尤其指貴重物品 <a hoard of cash>（大量現金），hoard作為動詞則是大量囤積的意思。

**i.e.** 請見e.g.。

**if; whether** 提供一個細微但實用的區別方法：if = 在此情況下。例如：Let me know if you need a catalog（如果需要目錄，敬請告知）。嚴格來說，這句話的含意是「如果不想要目錄，即無須告知」。whether = 詢問所做的決定。因此，Let me know whether you need a catalog（請告知是否需要目錄），嚴格來說，這句的意思是「無論要或不要，都請告知」。

**illegible** 請見eligible。

**illicit** 請見elicit。

**illusion** 請見allusion。

**imminent; eminent** imminent = 緊迫且無可避免<an imminent announcement>（緊急公告）。eminent = 著名且受尊敬的<an eminent authority on the subject>（此學科的著名權威）。

**impel** 請見compel。

**implicit** 請見explicit。

**imply; infer** imply = 暗示而不明說<There's an implied threat>（這帶有隱含的威脅）。infer = 推論<Can we infer from the announcement that they will build stores close to ours?>（根據公告內容可推論出他們會在我們的店附近蓋商店嗎？）。

**in behalf of** 請見on behalf of。

**incredulous** 請見credible。

**infer** 請見imply。

**ingenious; ingenuous** ingenious = 靈巧、巧妙的<That is an ingenious solution>（那是個很巧妙的解決方法）。ingenuous = 直率、純真、心無城府的<Security released the child, who they said was open and ingenuous under questioning>（保全說孩子在詢問過程中表現得坦率且真誠，因此把孩子放了）。

**in order to** 此片語一般可簡寫為to。只要不影響清楚表達，建議盡量使用簡寫的形式。

**insure** 請見assure。

**invoke** 請見evoke。

**irritate** 請見aggravate。

**it's; its** it's = it is <it's no mistake>（沒有錯）。its = it的所有格形式 <each branch has its responsibilities>（每個分行都有自己的職責）。

**jibe** 請見gibe。

**just deserts** （意指某人應得之物）應依此拼法拼寫，而不是*just desserts。deserve和desert [發音為[dɪˋzɜtʃ]為相關衍生字。

**lay > laid > laid** lay意為放置或佈置 <I'll lay it on his desk>（我會放在他的桌上）<I laid it on his desk yesterday>（我昨天已放在他的桌上）<if only I'd laid it there>（如果我有放在那裡）。

**lend; loan** lend = 提供、允許別人暫時使用 <Could you lend me that calculator?>（可以借我那個計算機嗎？）。loan = 借款 <We're paying back the loan>（我們會償還借款）。雖然一般多將loan當作名詞，但當受詞為金錢時，也可作為動詞 <We asked the bank to loan us $50,000>（我們向銀行借貸$50,000元）。

**less; fewer** less = 不可數名詞在數量上較少 <less waste>（較少浪費）。fewer = 可數名詞在數量上較少 <fewer losses>（較少損失）。

**lie > lay > lain** lie意指躺臥 <I should lie down>（我應該躺下）<I lay

down earlier this afternoon>（我下午稍早時躺了一下）<if I'd lain down this afternoon, I'd have more energy now>（如果我下午有躺一下，現在就會比較有精神）。

**like; as** like用在名詞或代名詞之前<like a rock>（像石頭一樣）。As用在主詞和動詞之前<as you said>（如你所說）。

**loan** 請見lend。

**loathe; loath** loathe為動詞，意為「厭惡」<He loathes broccoli>（他討厭花椰菜）。loath為形容詞，意為「不願意的」<He's loath to admit that he loves spinach>（他不願意承認自己愛吃菠菜）。

**loose; lose** loose為形容詞，意為「鬆的」或「不嚴謹的」<loose lips>（說溜嘴），亦可做動詞，意為「鬆開」<loose the dogs of war>（鬆開戰爭的獵犬，意指開始戰爭）。Lose為動詞<lose customers>（失去顧客），常被誤寫為loose。

**make do** = 勉強湊合<We'll have to make do with what's available>（我們只能以現有的資源勉強湊合）。此片語常被誤寫為*make due。

**marshal** 無論作為名詞<the fire marshal>（消防隊長），或動詞<marshal our arguments>（整理我們的論點），都是一樣的拼法。

**may** 請見can。

**mete out** = 分配。請依此拼法拼寫，勿寫作*meet out。

**militate** 請見 mitigate。

**minuscule** = 微小的<a minuscule amount>（微小的數量）。請依此拼

法拼寫，勿寫作*miniscule。

**mitigate; militate** mitigate = 使緩和<I normally would have filed a complaint, but there were mitigating circumstances>（通常我會提出投訴，但有一些原因使情況沒那麼嚴重）。militate = 對某方面有重大的影響<A long history of conflict militated against the agreement>（長久以來的衝突對協議造成不利影響）。

**mutual; common** mutual = 互相的<mutual admiration>（互相傾慕）。common = 共同的<common interests>（共同興趣）。

**nonplussed** = 過於驚訝而愣住，迷惑的<nonplussed by the shocking news>（因為令人震驚的消息而愣住）。

**number** 請見quantity。

**obtain** 請見attain。

**obtuse; abstruse** obtuse = 愚笨、遲鈍的<I was too obtuse to catch the allusion>（我太笨而聽不懂這個典故）。abstruse = 深奧難懂的<But it turns out that no one caught the abstruse allusion>（但結果沒人聽得懂這個深奧的典故）。

**on behalf of; in behalf of** on behalf of = 代表<accepting the award on behalf of>（代表領獎）。in behalf of = 支持<speaking in behalf of the motion>（發表談話支持此動議）。

**orient; *orientate** orient = 確定方位<spend the first day getting oriented>（第一天都在熟悉環境）。*orientate是較花俏的變體，應避免使用。

**past; passed** past可做名詞<in the past>（在以前）、形容詞<past efforts>（之前的努力）、副詞<walk on past>（走路經過）和介系詞<past the park>（經過公園）。Passed是動詞pass的過去式和過去分詞<time passed slowly>（時間過得很慢）。

**peak; peek; pique** peak = 最高點，尤其指山峰或圖表上波峰的尖端<reach the peak>（達到頂點）。peek = 偷偷的一瞥<take a peek at this file>（偷看這份檔案）。pique = (1)憤怒<a fit of pique>（一陣憤怒），或(2)激起<piqued her interest>（引起她的興趣）。

**peddle; pedal** peddle = 叫賣<peddle hot dogs>（叫賣熱狗）。pedal = 踩踏板<pedal a bike>（踩腳踏車）。

**peek** 請見peak。

**pejorative** = 帶有貶義、輕蔑的。請依此拼法拼寫，勿寫作*perjorative。

**pendant; pendent** pendant = 垂墜的吊飾<a silver pendant>（銀製墜飾）。pendent = 懸而未決的<a pendent lawsuit>（懸而未決的訴訟）。

**people** 請見persons。

**percent** 這個字的意思為「百分比」。以前的拼法為分開的兩個字，現在則拼為一個字。

**perquisite; prerequisite** perquisite = 特權或好處，尤其指因職位而獲得的津貼；多縮寫為perk <Perks included a company car>（津貼包括一輛公司配車）。prerequisite = 必備條件<This position has job-training prerequisites>（這個職位的必備條件是須完成工作訓練）。

**persecute; prosecute** persecute = 迫害，尤指針對某群體 <a persecuted minority>（受迫害的少數民族）。prosecute = 起訴 <prosecuted for embezzlement>（因貪污而遭起訴）。

**personal; personnel** personal = 形容詞，意為「私人的，個人的」。personnel = 名詞，意為「一間公司所聘僱的全體職員」。

**persuade** 請見convince。

**persons; people** 除了某些固定的短語外 <missing-persons report>（失蹤人口報告），在大多數情況下，用複數的persons聽來會有些生硬。應只將person用於單數型態 <Only one person showed up>（只有一個人出席），複數則用people。

**perspicuous; perspicacious** perspicuous = 清楚的 <a perspicuous argument>（清楚的論點）。perspicacious = 有洞察力的、精明的 <a perspicacious observer of the market>（精明的市場觀察家）。

**phase** 請見faze。

**pique** 請見peak。

**populace; populous** populace = 某個地方的全體居民 <the Swiss populace>（瑞士民眾）。populous = 人口稠密的 <populous northeastern cities>（東北方人口稠密的城市）。

**pore; pour** pore意指專心的研讀 <poring over the financial statements>（認真研讀財務報表）。pour意為讓液體傾瀉而下。

**practical; practicable** practical = 與經驗或實際應用有關的；因應實

際操作而調整，而不只是想法<There must be a practical way of shipping these goods>（一定有可運送這些商品的實際方法）。practicable = 可實行或可使用的<Scientists have long known that a perpetual-motion machine is impracticable>（科學家早就知道永動機是不可行的）。

**precede; proceed** precede = 發生在其他事之前<An extensive campaign preceded the launch>（在商品上市前，有大規模的行銷活動）。*preceed是常見的錯誤拼法。proceed = (1)開始<Proceed with your report>（開始你的報告），或(2)繼續<From St. Louis, proceed to Chicago>（從聖路易斯繼續前往芝加哥）。

**precipitate; precipitous** precipitate最常用作動詞，意為「使突然或猛然發生」<precipitate a riot>（引發一場暴動）。若作為形容詞，則是指「突然的、貿然的，或迅猛的」<a precipitate run on the banks>（突然在河岸邊跑了起來）。precipitous=陡峭的<a precipitous decline in demand>（需求急遽下降）。

**prerequisite** 請見 perquisite。

**prescribe; proscribe** prescribe = 給予指示<The consultants prescribed a plan>（顧問提出了一項方案）。proscribe = 禁止或限制<Insider trading is proscribed>（禁止內線交易）。

**presumptive; presumptuous** presumptive = 推定的<the presumptive nominee>（預期的被提名者）。presumptuous = 傲慢、放肆的<making presumptuous demands>（提出傲慢的要求）。

**preventive; *preventative** preventive = 防止傷害的<preventive measures>

（預防措施）。*preventative則是非正式的變體。

**principal; principle** principal = 主要的、首要的<the principal reason>（主要原因）。若作為名詞，則是指最主要的人<a principal at a consulting firm>（顧問公司的主要領導者）。在財務上，則指最初借出或投資的本金<the principal continues to earn interest>（本金可持續賺取利息）。principle = 信條、原則或定律 <stand on principle>（堅守原則）<the principles of economics>（經濟學原理）。

**proceed** 請見precede。

**prophesy; prophecy** prophesy = 預言（動詞）<prophesy great success>（預言可大獲成功）。prophecy = 預言（名詞）<another doomsday prophecy>（另一個末日預言）。

**proposition; proposal** proposition = 提出供對方考慮的建議<We reject the proposition that plants should be located only on rivers>（我們拒絕了應只將工廠建於河岸邊的建議）。proposal = 正式的提議<His proposal was silent on the personnel required to make it work>（他的提案並未提到負責執行的人員規劃）。

**proscribe** 請見prescribe。

**prosecute** 請見persecute。

**prostrate; prostate** prostrate = 俯臥的。prostate = 前列腺。

**proved; proven** proved = 長久以來，較多人偏好使用的prove的過去分詞<last year's projections have proved accurate>（已證明去年的預測準確），固定用語 innocent until proven guilty（證實有罪之前應推定

為無罪）則為例外。proven則是做形容詞用 <Our new line is already a proven seller>（新推出的系列已證實為暢銷商品）。

**purpose** 請見intention。

**quandary** = 困惑的狀態 <in a quandary about how to proceed>（對於如何繼續感到困惑），而非困惑的原因。

**quantity; number** quantity = 沒有確切數字的量 <The farm produces large quantities of grain>（這個農場生產大量的穀物）。number = 個別可數物件的總量 <The number of units we sold last year exceeded that of any previous year>（去年賣出的件數超過以往任何一年的數量）。

**rack** 請見wrack。

**rebut; refute** rebut = 回應某個指控或論點。refute = 反駁某個指控或論點。

**reek; wreak** reek = (1)發臭 <The stagnant water reeks>（靜止的水發出臭味），或(2)惡臭 <We could smell the reek of an open sewer>（我們可聞到開放排水管傳出的惡臭）。wreak = 造成特定類型的傷害 <wreak havoc>（造成巨大災害）。

**refute** 請見rebut。

**regrettable; regretful** regrettable = 不幸的 <a regrettable decision>（令人遺憾的決定）。regretful = 後悔的 <regretful about not calling>（後悔未打電話）。

**rein; reign** rein = 馬轡的韁繩，可比喻為用於控制的方式 <give free

rein>（放任自由）<to rein in>（約束）。同音字reign（=統治）有時會被誤用於上述用語和其他類似用語中。

**relegate; delegate** relegate = 重新指派較低的職位或工作<relegated to traffic control>（貶職至交通管制）。delegate = 委派（某人）為代表<delegated the research to Terry>（將研究工作委派給泰瑞）。

**reluctant** 請見reticent。

**respectfully; respectively** respectfully = 恭敬有禮的<May I respectfully ask you to wait another five minutes>（我能否恭敬的請您再等五分鐘）。respectively = 依序分別為<So $500,000 and $600,000 are the benchmarks, respectively, for Ted and Carol>（泰德和凱蘿的基準分別是$500,000和$600,000）。

**reticent; reluctant** reticent = 沉默寡言、不輕易表露想法、不願交談的<Veterans can be reticent about their experiences>（老兵有可能不願意提起過去的經歷）。請勿將這個字與reluctant（不情願的）搞混，例如：reluctant to act（不情願的採取動作）。

**role; roll** role（意為「在組織中的職責、電影中的角色」等）和roll（意為「參與者、演員等等之類的名單」）經常會被搞混。

**sanction** = (1)處罰<The commission imposed sanctions for the incident>（委員會對此事件祭出了制裁），或(2)許可<The board gave its sanction for continued talks>（董事會准許繼續對談）。

**species; specie** species = 植物或動物的物種，單複數同形。specie= 硬幣。

**stanch** 請見staunch。

**stationary; stationery** stationary = 靜止的 <The gym has five stationary bikes>（健身房有五部健身腳踏車）。stationery = 信紙 <We received 12 boxes of stationery>（我們收到了十二箱信紙）。

**staunch; stanch** staunch = 忠實堅定的 <He's a staunch supporter>（他是忠實的支持者）。stanch = 止住或控制以防止液體流出，也可用於比喻性的用法<stanch the red ink>（不讓紅色墨水流出）。

**strait; straight** strait = 狹窄的水道，亦比喻困境<Strait of Magellan>（麥哲倫海峽）<in dire straits>（陷入困境）。在拼寫straitjacket和straitlaced時，常會以straight取代strait。

**strategy; tactics** strategy = 整體的規劃<competitive strategy>（有競爭力的策略）。tactics = 為整體規劃提供支援的行動和技巧<flash mobs and other guerrilla-marketing tactics>（快閃活動和其他游擊行銷戰略）。

**subsequent** 請見consequent。

**supersede** = 取代<It supersedes last year's employee handbook>（它取代了去年的員工手冊）。這個字常被拼錯成*supercede。

**sympathy** 請見empathy。

**tactics** 請見strategy。

**than** 請見then。

**that; which** 用that來引導補充必要資訊的子句（限定子句），且無須以逗號分隔。如果你說“The departments that made their numbers last quarter received budget increases”（上一季達成預定目標的部門，預算都獲得增加），讀者會認為有些部門的預算沒有增加。引導非必要的子句（非限定子句）時，則應該用which。如果你說“The departments, which made their numbers last quarter, received budget increases”（各部門上一季都達成了預定目標，預算也都獲得增加。），是表示所有部門的預算都有增加。如果將以逗號分隔的which子句拿掉，仍可表達這句話的主要意思。

**their** 請見there。

**then; than** then = 當時；那麼；所以。than則用於表示比較 <more successful than any other start-up>（比其他所有新創公司都更成功）。

**there; their; they're** there用於指示方向 <over there>（在那裡），或地方 <where there is life>（在有生命的地方）；their是they的所有格 <all their worldly belongings>（他們所有的物質財產）；they're是they are的縮讀字 <they're on the way>（他們已經在路上）。

**torpid** 請見turgid。

**toward; towards** 美式英語大多用toward，英式英語則多用towards。

**try and** 建議應用try to。

**turgid; torpid** turgid = (1)膨脹的 <the turgid river after Friday's rain>（週五大雨過後，水勢暴漲的河流），或(2)浮誇的 <a turgid harangue>（浮誇的長篇大論）。torpid = 沉睡的或遲緩的 <Demand is usually torpid after the holidays>（假期過後，需求通常較為遲緩）。

**uninterested** 請見disinterested。

**unique; unusual** unique = 獨一無二、無可比擬的 <a unique handmade quilt>（獨一無二的手工棉被）。unique本身已隱含絕對的概念，因此不應再與very等修飾語連用。unique與unusual並非同義字。

**use; utilize** 建議選用較簡單的字。

**venal; venial** venal = 腐敗、受賄的 <a venal border guard>（腐敗的邊境警衛）。venial = 可原諒的 <a venial mistake>（可原諒的錯誤）。

**veracity; voracity** veracity = 真實 <Veracity earns trust>（真實才能贏得信任）。voracity = 貪食、貪婪 <His voracity was his downfall>（貪婪使他墮落）。

**verbiage** = 冗詞贅句，而不是指訊息中的文字，因此excess verbiage這樣的說法是多餘的。請勿將此字錯拼成*verbage。

**vocation; avocation** vocation = 職業 <His vocation is nursing>（他的職業是看護）。Avocation = (1)愛好，或(2)副業 <On weekends he works on his avocation, flint-knapping>（他在週末從事打磨燧石工具的業餘愛好）。

**voluminous** 請見compendious。

**voracity** 請見veracity。

**wangle** 請見wrangle。

**whether** 請見if。

**whether; whether or not** 在多數情況下，whether都可單獨存在，是否有or not並不影響意思。但在表達「無論是否」的意思時，則必須加上or not<We're going whether or not you can make it>（無論你是否能來，我們都會去）。

**which** 請見that。

**who's; whose** who's = who is。whose = who或whom的所有格形式。

**whosever; whoever's** whosever是whoever的標準所有格形式。whoever's是whoever is的縮讀字。

**workers' compensation** 這個中性的用語已經取代workmen's compensation成為標準用法。

**wrack; rack** wrack= (1)毀壞<wracked by fraud>（因詐騙而陷於困境），或(2)殘骸<go to wrack and ruin>（變得殘破不堪）。rack = 像在刑架上受苦一般<rack my brains>（絞盡腦汁）。

**wrangle; wangle** wrangle = 大聲的爭吵<wrangling over licensing rights>（為授權權利爭吵）。wangle = 用計獲得<wangle an invitation>（設法獲得邀請）。

**wreak** 請見reek。

**your; you're** your = you的所有格。you're = you are的縮讀字。

• NOTE •

# 建議參考書目

好的寫作能力不僅只是單一技能，而是多種不同技能的整合——更是一門必須持續不斷學習的學問。除了本書之外，建議可將以下書籍備於案頭，以便隨時參考。

## 寫作者基本參考書目


- The American Heritage Dictionary of the English Language. 5th ed. Boston: Houghton Mifflin Harcourt, 2011.
- Garner, Bryan A. Garner's Dictionary of Modern American Usage. 3d ed. New York: Oxford, 2009.
- Merriam-Webster's Collegiate Dictionary. 11th ed. Springfield, MA: Merriam-Webster, 2008.
- Roget's Thesaurus of English Words and Phrases. George Davidson, ed. Avon, MA: Adams Media, 2011.
- Trimble, John R. Writing with Style. 3d ed. Upper Saddle River, NJ: Pearson, 2010.

## 行家級進階參考書目


- Flesch, Rudolf. The Art of Plain Talk. New York: Harper & Brothers, 1946.
- Flesch, Rudolf. How to Write Plain English: A Book for Lawyers and Consumers. New York: Harper & Row, 1979.
- Fowler, H. W. A Dictionary of Modern English Usage. 2d ed. Edited by Ernest Gowers. New York: Oxford University Press, 1965.
- Garner, Bryan A. Legal Writing in Plain English. 2d ed. Chicago: University of Chicago Press, 2012.
- Gowers, Ernest. The Complete Plain Words. 3d ed. Edited by Sidney Greenbaum and Janet Whitcut. Boston: David R. Godine, 1986.
- Graves, Robert, and Alan Hodge. The Reader over Your Shoulder. 2d ed. London: Cape, 1947.
- Partridge, Eric. Usage and Abusage: A Guide to Good English. New York: Harper & Brothers, 1942.
- Strunk, William, and E. B. White. The Elements of Style. 4th ed. Boston: Allyn & Bacon, 1999.
- Tufte, Edward R. Beautiful Evidence. Cheshire, Conn.: Graphics Press, 2006.
- Tufte, Edward R. Envisioning Information. Cheshire, Conn.: Graphics Press, 1990.
- Wallace, David Foster. Consider the Lobster. New York: Little, Brown & Co., 2005.
- Zinsser, William. On Writing Well. New York: HarperCollins, 30th Ann. ed., 2006.

# 索引


acronyms 縮寫, 121
adverbs 副詞, 191-192, 194-195
all caps 全部大寫, 211
Alred, Gerald J. 傑拉德J.阿爾德, 155
*and*, starting a sentence with 以 and 做為句子開頭, 190
apostrophes, improper use of 撇號，不恰當的使用, 200-201
appositives 同位語, 196-197, 201
Architect phase 建築師階段, 28-31, 34, 186
articles, (*a, an, the*) don't drop 冠詞，不可省略, 66
*as per*, 73, 77, 138, 140
*attached please find*, 77
audience 目標讀者、受眾
    connecting with 鎖定, 23-24, 100
    for letters 對於信件, 16-20
    holding readers' attention 抓住讀者的注意力, 114-121
    motivating to act 鼓勵採取行動, 147-150
    nonspecialists 非專業人士, 24, 58
    perspective of 角度, 56, 151
    understanding readers 了解目標讀者, 22-26
    who you're writing for 誰是你的目標對象？ 23-24

Babenroth, A. Charles A. 查爾斯貝本若斯, 154-155
Bartholomew, Wallace E. 華萊士E.巴塞洛繆, 154
*Beautiful Evidence* (Tufte), 52, 245
*be* verbs  be動詞, 68, 118
bizspeak 商務用語, 72-82
boilerplate 制式用語, 77
boldface type 粗體字, 203
brainstorming 腦力激盪, 29-30, 33-34
brevity and clarity 簡潔與清晰, 23, 41, 57-58, 94, 106, 160-161
Brusaw, Charles T. 查爾斯T.布魯索, 155
Buffett, Warren 華倫巴菲特, 23-24, 78-82
bullets, as attention-getting device 項目符號，為吸引注意力的工具, 202
*but*, starting a sentence with 以 but 做為句子開頭, 190
buzzwords 流行語, 72-75

Cannon, Kelly 凱利卡農, 155
Carpenter phase 木匠階段, 28-29, 31, 36-43, 187
*Chicago Manual of Style, The*, 30, 199
chronology 按事件發生的先後順序排列, 84-87
Churchill, Winston 邱吉爾, 114
clarity 清楚明瞭, 56-61, 66
clichés 過度濫用的詞句, 73-75
closing text 結語, 42, 44-45
Cordy, Sherwin 舒爾文科迪, 154
collegiality 合作友好的態度, 123-124
colons 冒號, 202-204
commas 逗號, 190, 194, 196, 199-200, 203-204
conclusions, leading readers to 引導讀者自行得出結論, 58

concrete writing 具體的寫作, 61
conjunctions 連接詞
correlative 相關連接詞, 193, 197
starting sentences with 句子以…開頭, 105-106, 190
connecting with large audiences 鎖定一大群目標對象, 23-25
continuity and transitions 連貫性和轉折, 88-94, 190
contractions 縮讀字, 116-117, 200
courtesy 保持禮貌, 20, 156
credibility 公信力, 64, 98, 101

dates 日期, 204, 211
definitions 定義, 58, 163
delivering bad news 傳達壞消息, 150-153
dialect 方言, 103-104
diplomacy 圓融, 156-157
double negatives 雙重否定, 103
drafts 草稿
e-mail 電子郵件, 130-136
feedback 提供意見, 108-110
first 初稿, 13, 30-31
revising 修改, 44-50
writing rapidly 快速的寫, 42-43
Drucker, Peter 彼得杜拉克, 43
dumbing it down 簡化內容, 81

editing 編輯, 31, 45
efficiency 最高效率, 29
*either*, 100-102, 193
*Elements of Style, The* (Strunk and White)《英文寫作風格的要素》, 204, 245
e-mails 電子郵件
BCC 密件副本, 211
check before sending 寄出前檢查, 210
general guidelines for 一般準則, 128-136
storytelling 陳述事件, 84-87
subject line 信件主旨, 129, 211
em-dashes 長破折號, 203
emphasis, adding 增加強調, 52-53, 202-204
empty words 空泛的詞語, 24-25
*enclosed please find*, 138, 140, 454-155
*Envisioning Information* (Tufte), 52, 245
etiquette, business writing 禮儀，商業寫作, 210-212

feedback from colleagues 來自同事的意見, 108-110
Flesch Reading Ease (FRE) scale 弗雷奇易讀性指數(FRE), 80
Flesch, Rudolf 魯道夫弗雷奇, 80, 115
Flowers, Betty Sue 貝蒂蘇佛勞爾絲, 28-29
focus 重點
finding it 找出來, 32-41
"you" focus 用「你」當重點, 115-116, 133, 139, 145
fonts 字體, 200
forms of address 稱謂方式, 210
Frailey, L.E. 佛萊利L. E., 155
FRE scale 弗雷奇易讀性指數, 80
fund-raising 募款, 147-149

genderless pronouns 無性別代名詞, 101
getting to the point 點出重點, 22
*good and well*, 191-192, 206
grammar 文法
generally 常見文法問題96-106

mistakes creating bad impressions 錯誤用法造成壞印象, 206-208
passive voice 被動語態, 118-119, 146
phrasal adjectives 形容詞短語, 198-199
rules to know 需要了解的規則, 96-106
graphics 圖表, 52-54

*Harvard Law Review*《哈佛法律評論》, 81
*however*, 105-106, 190, 194
Hurlbut, Floyd 弗洛伊德赫爾伯特, 154
hyperformality compared to polished plain speech 非常正式與修飾過的平實文字, 75-76, 122-123
hyphens 連字號, 198, 203

impressions, bad 留下壞印象, 206-208
"index expurgatorius"「禁用字目錄」, 72-75
inspiration 靈感, 43
*-ion* words–ion 結尾的名詞, 68
issues, stating plainly 問題，直陳重點, 16, 62-64, 161-163, 165-167
italic type, for emphasis 斜體表達強調, 200, 202-203

Judge phase 法官階段, 28-29, 31, 42-43, 187-188

letters 信件
as a tool for sharpening writing skills 透過寫信來磨練技能, 60
chronology in 依時間順序說明, 84-87
form and purpose 形式與目的, 16-20
general guidelines for 一般準則, 138-158
replying to 回信, 211
salutations 稱呼語, 203, 210
signature 簽署, 210
Dos and Don'ts 注意事項, 210-212
logic 邏輯, 30, 32
long dashes, uses for 長破折號功用 197, 203-204

MACJ, 28-29, 43
Madman phase 狂人階段, 28-31, 33-34, 43, 186
Madman–Architect–Carpenter–Judge 狂人－建築師－木匠－法官, 28-29
main points 主要重點, 32-41
marketing reports 行銷報告, 164-168
memos 備忘錄, 12, 23, 33-41, 45-50, 160-168
middle 正文, 42, 44-45, 160, 162-164
mistakes, admitting 勇於承認錯誤, 151
motivating readers 激勵目標讀者, 147-150

*neither*, 100, 102, 193-194, 197
nonstandard language 非標準詞彙, 104-105
notes, making 作筆記, 30
nouns 名詞
disagreement with pronouns 與代名詞不一致, 101-102
plural 複數, 200-201

*of*, 68-69
Oliu, Walter E. 奧利烏沃爾特 E., 155
opening text 導言, 42, 44

opinions, unsupported 沒有任何論點支持的意見, 58, 61
organizing 組織
chronology 依先後順序陳述事情, 84-87
main points/issues and logic 主要重點／問題和邏輯, 32 41
outlining 大綱, 30, 64
sets of three 三個, 32-41
subheads 副標題, 93-94
*otherwise*, 194
outlining 大綱, 30, 64

padding, recognizing and eliminating 贅詞辨識與刪除, 66-70
paragraph openers 段落開頭, 88-90
passive voice 被動語態, 118-119, 146
performance appraisals 績效考核表, 170-184
persuasiveness 有說服力, 3, 61, 139-140
phrasal adjectives, hyphenating 形容詞短語 連字號, 198-199
phrases 用語
canned 制式、公式化, 77, 138, 140-141, 154-155
creating bad impressions 給人不好的印象, 206-208
overused 過度濫用, 73-75
for performance reviews 員工評鑑用, 170-184
plagiarism 抄襲, 30
plain-spoken language, importance of 用字簡單直接的重要性, 72-82
planning your writing project 計畫寫作項目, 28-41
polishing your writing 修改寫作, 29, 31, 76, 109-110
possessives 所有格, 204-205
predicates, compound 複合謂語, 199-200
prefixes, hyphenating 字首連字號, 203
prepositions 介系詞, 68, 97, 99, 190-191, 192-193
*prior to*, 66
process of writing 寫作過程, 28-43
procrastination 停滯不前, 43
pronouns 代名詞
errors in using 錯誤用法, 96-97, 101-102
personal 人稱代名詞, 115-116, 123
relative 關係代名詞, 195-195
punctuation, basic rules of 標點符號的基本規則, 194, 196-197, 198-205
purpose for writing 寫作的目的, 16-20

quotation marks for emphasis 用引號來強調, 202-203

readers. *See also* audience 目標讀者
nonspecialist 非專業人士, 24, 58
perspective 角度, 56, 151
three types for memos 摘要內容是為了三種讀者而寫, 163
time constraints 時間限制, 22-23
understanding 了解他們, 22-26
*Reader's Digest* 讀者文摘, 81
reason for writing 寫作原因，請參見 purpose for writing
recommendations 建議, 164-168
rejection 拒絕, 150-153
relative pronouns 所有格代名詞, 195-196

reports, tips on writing 撰寫報告的技巧, 160-168
reprimand by e-mail 透過電子郵件訓誡, 133-136
requests for proposal 客戶的提案要求, 23
research 蒐集素材, 29-31, 164
reviews, employee 員工評鑑，請參見 performance appraisals
revising 修改內容
    general guidelines for 一般準則, 44-50
    continuity and transitions 連貫性和轉折, 88-94

salutations, punctuation following 稱呼語後的標點符號, 203
sarcasm 諷刺的語氣, 124-125, 202
semicolons 分號, 194, 199-200, 203
sentences 句子
    compound subjects 複合主詞, 192-193
    conjunctions at beginning of 連接詞在句首, 105-106, 190
    length of 長度, 57-58, 78-82
    noun–pronoun disagreement 名詞與代名詞不一致, 101-102
    prepositions at end of 介系詞在句尾, 190-191
    pronouns 代名詞, 96-97, 101-102, 115-116
    starters 開頭, 105-106, 190
    structure 結構, 119-120
    subject–verb disagreement 主詞動詞不一致, 98-100
"Show, don't tell," 要具體呈現，不要只是空洞描述。58-61
signature 簽名檔、署名, 129, 210
simplicity and clarity in language 用字簡潔清楚, 56-61, 66-70, 72-82, 114, 117
sources 資料來源, 30
speed writing 快寫, 31, 42-43
split infinitives 分離不定詞, 195
standard English 標準英語, 104-105
starting to write 埋頭苦寫, 28-41
storytelling and chronology 陳述事情經過並依先後順序, 84-87
Strunk, William, Jr. 史壯克與懷特, 204, 245
style, how to acquire good 如何學習好的寫作風格, 10-13
subheads 副標題, 93-94, 211
subject lines 信件主旨, 129, 160-161, 211
subject–verb agreement 主詞動詞一致, 98-100, 102, 192-194
summarizing 摘要, 62-65, 94, 160-168

*thank you in advance*, 78, 211
thank-you notes 感謝函, 60, 211
*that*, 66, 195-196, 239-240
*there*, 98-99, 240
*their*, 101-102, 240
*therefore*, 93, 194
third person 第三人稱, 116
*Time* (magazine)《時代雜誌》, 81
time management 時間管理, 42-44
titles 標題, 160-161
tone 語氣
    collegial 友好的, 115-116, 123-124
    combative 好鬥的, 156-157
    courteous and direct 禮貌且直接的, 157
    in e-mails 在電子郵件中, 130-136
    friendly 友善的, 17, 60, 123-124, 157

hyperformality 過度正式, 122-125
purpose and content 目的與內容, 16-20, 22-23
relaxed 輕鬆的, 122-123
sarcasm 諷刺, 124-125, 202
stern 嚴厲的, 20
urgent 緊急的, 16-20
transitions and continuity 過渡與連貫, 88-94
Tufte, Edward, 52, 245

underlining 使用底線, 202
U.S. Securities and Exchange Commission's *Plain English Handbook* 美國證券交易委員會的《Plain English Handbook》, 23
usage 用法
bad examples of 錯誤示範, 206-208
good 正確示範, 214-242

vagueness 含糊不清, 56, 61, 64, 140
verbs 動詞
irregular 不規則, 105
past-tense 過去式, 118
separating the grammatical subject from 將語法主詞分開, 201
split infinitives 分離不定詞, 195
strong 較有力的, 68-69
verb phrases 動詞詞組, 195
visual aids 視覺輔助素材, 52-53
vocabulary 詞彙, 104-105

Washington, George 華盛頓, 114
*we*, 97, 115, 123, 146-147
*well*, 191-192, 206
*which*, 195-196
White, E. B. 懷特, 204, 245
White, Richard Grant 理查德格蘭特懷特, 154
white space in document design 檔案設計中的空白, 210-211
*who*, 195-196, 205
"who, what, when, where, and why,"的用法, 53, 64
wordiness, controlling 控制贅字, 66-70
wording, problems with 文字運用問題, 96-106
words, wasting of 拒絕贅字, 96-106
writer's block 寫作瓶頸, 30, 41, 43
writing 寫作
anxiety about 焦慮, 28-30
benefits of good writing 擅長寫作的益處, 8-13
etiquette in 禮儀, 210-212
four stages checklist for 四階段的檢查清單, 186-188
how to begin 如何下筆, 28-41
process of 過程, 28-43
purpose of 目的, 16-20
rapidly 快速, 42-43
style 風格, 114-125
timing 計時, 42

"you" focus 以目標讀者為中心, 115-116, 133, 139, 147

# 致謝

謹在此向以下各位表達最誠摯的感謝。首先是《哈佛商業評論》的麗莎布瑞爾(Lisa Burrell)，此書是在她的建議下出版，並在她的手中經過多次修訂校對。感謝LawProse的員工Heather C. Haines、Becky R. McDaniel、Tiger Jackson、Jeff Newman、David Zheng和Ryden McComas Anderson，多虧有他們幫忙發想和修改文字。感謝在X追蹤我的用戶（X的前身為推特，我的帳號是@bryanagarner），他們提供了應避免使用的商務用語建議。感謝我的岳母Sandra W. Cheng、岳母的哥哥Daniel Wu，以及我的嫂嫂Linda Garner，他們憑藉自己在商業領域多年的經驗，提供了一些值得深入探索的建議。最後，我最要感謝的是我的妻子Karolyne H.C. Garner，在我寫這本書的那幾個月，她一如既往的鼓勵我、激勵我，並為我加油。

我要將這本書獻給電影製片人J.P. Allen，他是我從小到大的好朋友（初識時，我五歲，他三歲）。到了十幾歲時，我們開始對語言和寫作感興趣，同時也熱切的閱讀關於創業和企業管理的書籍，從來不擔心可能會成為別人眼中的怪胎或書呆子。那時的我們認為學習是一件很酷的事，無知才真的遜，至今我們仍這麼相信。

B.A.G.

2012年8月

# 關於作者

布萊恩A.賈納(Bryan A. Garner)是著名的詞典編纂者、語法學家、律師，也是一家公司的負責人。自1991年建立LawProse Inc.以來，他已訓練超過150,000名律師，傳授如何以書面文字說服他人和有效撰寫契約的技巧，包括幾十家《財富》世界500強企業的法務部門都是他的客戶。

賈納著有《Garner's Modern American Usage》、《The Elements of Legal Style》和《The Winning Brief》等書，也是各版已出版的《布萊克法律字典》(Black's Law Dictionary)的總編，並與法官安東寧史卡利亞(Antonin Scalia)合著了兩本關於法院審理判決的暢銷書。

EZ TALK

# 哈佛商業評論
# 英文商務寫作權威指南

作　　者：布萊恩 A. 賈納 Bryan A. Garner
譯　　者：賴榮鈺
執行編輯：潘亭軒
審　　訂：Judd Piggott
封面設計：水青子
版型設計：水青子
內頁排版：水青子
行銷企劃：張爾芸

發 行 人：洪祺祥
副總經理：洪偉傑
副總編輯：曹仲堯
法律顧問：建大法律事務所
財務顧問：高威會計事務所

出　　版：日月文化出版股份有限公司
製　　作：EZ 叢書館
地　　址：臺北市信義路三段 151 號 8 樓
電　　話：(02) 2708-5509
傳　　真：(02) 2708-6157
網　　址：www.heliopolis.com.tw
郵撥帳號：19716071 日月文化出版股份有限公司

總 經 銷：聯合發行股份有限公司
電　　話：(02) 2917-8022
傳　　真：(02) 2915-7212
客服信箱：service@heliopolis.com.tw
印　　刷：中原造像股份有限公司
初　　版：2025 年 7 月
定　　價：400 元
I S B N：978-626-7641-69-9

哈佛商業評論英文商務寫作權威指南 / 布萊恩 A. 賈納 (Bryan A. Garner) 著；賴榮鈺譯 . -- 初版 . -- 臺北市：日月文化出版股份有限公司 , 2025.07
256 面；14.8×21 公分 . -- (EZ talk)
譯自：HBR Guide to Better Business Writing
ISBN 978-626-7641-69-9 ( 平裝 )
1.CST: 商業英文 2.CST: 商業應用文
3.CST: 寫作法

805.18　　114006956